THE HAND OF FEAR

Millionaire Felix Dexon left his London hotel one morning and never returned. Then his American lawyers began to receive hand-written instructions from him to regularly transfer large sums of money abroad, with the cheques made out to himself. The letters and cheques were confirmed as genuine by handwriting experts. But when his suspicious niece asks a London newspaper to try and find her uncle, their chief crime reporter uncovers a vast web of intrigue by a criminal mastermind responsible for a series of horrific murders . . .

GERALD VERNER

THE HAND OF FEAR

Complete and Unabridged

LINFORD
Leicester

First published in Great Britain

First Linford Edition
published 2015

A catalogue record for this book is available
from the British Library.

ISBN 978–1–4448–2305–9

1885484 21

Published by
F. A. Thorpe (Publishing)
Anstey, Leicestershire

Set by Words & Graphics Ltd.
Anstey, Leicestershire
Printed and bound in Great Britain by
T. J. International Ltd., Padstow, Cornwall

This book is printed on acid-free paper

1

The Tramp

The Deneswood Valley Estate lies in the shadow of the Surrey Hills between Redhill arid Bletchingly. The approach from the main road is by way of a broad gravel boulevard flanked by trees and guarded at its entrance by a decorative signpost bearing the inscription 'Private Road', for the residents of the estate are a retiring people and not partial to strangers.

Mr. Ambrose Blessington, to whose wide dreams and indefatigable work the place owed its inception, set out with the intention of creating a miniature garden city not too far from London, amid the most picturesque surroundings it was possible to obtain, where well-to-do businessmen and others could settle down and live in such peace as the limitations of their bank balances allowed. That Mr. Blessington had succeeded in his objective was testified to by the fact that not one of the score or so of houses, whose gables and twisted chimneys peeped from among the trees that enclosed them, was unoccupied. This was certainly not surprising, for a more beautiful spot than Deneswood Valley would have been difficult to find. None of the stereotyped architecture of the 'jerry builder' had been allowed to intrude into this Edenistic paradise. Each house was a design unto itself, passed only after much thought and care on the part of Mr. Blessington, who had superintended the building of each one personally, being careful to reject all materials that were not of the very best, and exercising much care in the laying out of the extensive gardens in which each residence was sited.

The houses were set at irregular intervals from each other so that there was nothing in the nature of a formulaic pattern to offend the artistic soul of Mr. Blessington. They were built round a central park — a flat, smooth stretch of emerald grass with a border of well-rolled gravel, and laid out with flowerbeds that blazed from May to October. In a far corner was a fluttering red pennant which indicated the first tee of the golf course that stretched away down the valley, and was exclusive to the residents of the estate and their various friends. Here, too, were the five tennis courts, their white markings sharp and clear, their nets tightly stretched — models of what tennis courts should be.

From the study windows of his own house — for he lived in the big grey stone mansion at the end of the winding approach — Mr. Blessington could see the white-clad figures playing, and when he allowed his eyes to wander over the beauties of the scene that stretched before him, there came to him a feeling of that joy which is only experienced by the creator.

The garden city was very select. Mr. Blessington had taken the utmost pains in picking its tenants and many applicants had been politely turned down, to their surprise and chagrin, with the barest of formal refusals, and no explanation as to the reason, merely because they did not fit in with Mr. Blessington's plan. The rents were high — that was only to be expected for such advantages as the estate offered — and were paid directly to Mr. Blessington himself exactly on each quarter-day.

He acted as his own estate agent, and he never had any trouble. Deneswood Valley was a rich community. The incomes of its residents, if added together, would have totalled a sum running into seven figures.

Strolling along the smooth gravel walk that flanked the central garden and admiring the beauty which a hot summer's afternoon gave to the child of his brain, Mr. Blessington felt very contented with the world.

He was a man whose age might have been anything between forty-five and sixty. His big, smooth face was unlined, and his gait was alert to the verge of briskness. He was fat, but he carried his stoutness so well that it was scarcely noticeable at first glance. He raised his soft grey hat to a slim girl in white who, with a racket under her arm, came out of a nearby house and crossed over to the green. She gave him a smile as she passed, and he continued his walk with a face that had suddenly become grave and thoughtful.

Rounding a clump of gaily hued shrubs, Mr. Blessington received something of a shock. Coming towards him was the untidy figure of a man — an ill-dressed, ragged man, with a growth of thick stubble on his chin and dusty spots that gaped at the toes.

'Bless my soul!' murmured Mr. Blessington in horror. The very thought of a tramp in that beautiful setting was abhorrent to his artistic nature.

The ragged man drew nearer, and as he came level, stopped. ''ere, Guv'nor, p'r'aps you can 'elp me,' he said quickly, swaying slightly on his feet. 'Want to find a feller. Sam Gates, 'is name is. Lives round 'ere somewhere.' He waved a dirty hand vaguely.

Mr. Blessington inwardly shuddered. A tramp was bad enough, but a drunken tramp! 'I think you've made a mistake, my good man — ' he began majestically, but the tramp interrupted with an unsteady laugh.

'I ain't made no mistake, ol' feller,' he said. 'Oh, no, I ain't made no mistake. I've come to see Sam Gates, an' I'm blinking well goin' ter see 'im.'

'There is nobody of that name here,' asserted Mr. Blessington with dignity. 'Now, you just go away quietly, or I shall have to call the gardener and have you put off the estate.'

The tramp eyed him unpleasantly. 'Call the gardener, will you?' he snarled. 'All right. Go on then — call your gardener, you fat old slug! I ain't a-goin' from 'ere till I've seen Sam, see?'

Mr. Blessington breathed a trifle hard, but decided that perhaps the situation could be met by the use of a little tact. 'I have already told you,' he said in his most dignified manner, 'that there is nobody here of the name of Gates. I know all the servants and I can vouch for the fact that there is none of them with that name.'

'Who said anythin' about servants?' The ragged man leaned forward and gripped Mr. Blessington's immaculate grey sleeve with a greasy hand. 'You don't know wot you're talkin' about. Sam Gates ain't no blinkin' servant. He's a pal o' mine, and I don't 'ssociate with servants, see? Sam's got an 'ouse 'ere. One o' them.' He jerked his head towards the houses half-revealed through the trees.

Mr. Blessington took his arm away and shook his own head. 'You're come to the wrong place, my man,' he said sternly. 'This is the Deneswood Valley Estate, and there is nobody living here or otherwise with the name of Gates.'

'I know this is the Deneswood Ish-Ishtate,' said the tramp with difficulty, 'an' I know of Sam's 'ere too. It ain't no good you tryin' to put me off with lot o' lies. I got it straight from Tyler, see? No, you jest move yourself an' show me which is ol' Sam's house.'

Mr. Blessington looked round nervously and gave a sigh of relief as he saw the gardener approaching. Really, it was intolerable that he should have been waylaid in this manner. Already abusive, the man was fast becoming threatening.

'I shall not argue with you further,' he

said. 'I can only conclude that you are mad or the drink you have consumed has affected your — er — brain. Now, I don't want any unpleasantness, but unless you go quietly and at once, I shall have to have you removed by force.'

The tramp's thick lips curled back in a savage snarl, revealing his broken, tobacco-stained teeth. 'Oh, yer will, will yer,' he cried hoarsely. 'Go on, you just try it, you old — ! I'll knock yer bloomin' face through the other side of yer 'ead!'

He clenched his fists, and Mr. Blessington took a hasty step backwards, and then suddenly the tramp's temper subsided, and his voice dropped to a conciliatory whine. 'All right, Guv'nor, I'll go. Didn't mean no 'arm,' he muttered, and shuffled off in the direction of the main road.

Mr. Blessington gasped his relief and looked round to see what had caused this sudden change of front on the part of the unpleasant trespasser. But there was no one in sight except the gardener. Apparently the tramp had altered his mind of his own volition. Well, anyway — Mr. Blessington watched the ragged

8

figure turn into the private road and disappear round a bend — he was gone.

A most objectionable man, he thought as he walked slowly back to his house for tea, and not only objectionable but dangerous. He decided to speak to the police about the matter, and then immersing himself in some work that awaited him that evening, the episode of the tramp passed for the moment from his mind. Mr. Blessington was an early riser and he had just descended to his breakfast on the following morning when his servant announced that the head gardener wished to see him urgently. He went out and found the agitated and white-faced man waiting nervously in the hall.

'Well, what is it, Jennings?' asked Mr. Blessington.

'Something dreadful has happened,' said the old man tremulously. 'Will you come with me, sir? I thought I'd better tell you at once — before anyone found it.'

'Found it — found what?' demanded Mr. Bleasington a little irritably. He was never at his best before breakfast.

'The — the body, sir,' whispered the gardener hoarsely, and his master jumped.

'What do you mean? Is someone dead?' he exclaimed, and Jennings nodded his grey head.

'Yes, sir — I think it's murder!' he said. 'If you'll come with me, sir, I'll show you.'

'Murder? Good heavens!' Mr. Blessington's eyes started from his head. 'Yes, yes, show me at once!'

He followed the gardener down the drive and out onto the gravelled walk. It was fresh and cool in the early morning sunlight.

'Here, sir,' said Jennings, and stopping beside a clump of bushes, pointed downwards. 'Look, sir!'

Mr. Blessington looked, and his large face went the colour of chalk. Stretched on his back, his sightless eyes turned to the sky, and his ragged coat stiff with the blood that had welled from the wound in his throat, lay the figure of the tramp who had accosted him the previous afternoon.

'He's been stabbed in the neck, sir,' muttered Jennings tremulously, 'and there's no sign of a knife anywhere, so I suppose it must have been murder, sir.'

Mr. Blessington recovered himself with an effort. 'That's a matter for the police to find out,' he said. 'We must send for them at once.' And then an afterthought struck him: 'Good heavens! The publicity of this crime will be horrible — horrible!'

Could he have looked into the future he would have found good cause for his remark, for the murder of tramp was but the beginning, and was shortly to be followed by a series of events that were to make the Deneswood Valley world notorious, obscuring its peace and beauty beneath a mantle of mystery, fear and sudden death.

2

Farringdon Street

Mr. Farringdon Street came leisurely down the Strand, his hands in his pockets, his lips pursed on a whistle that was soundless. His bearing held a touch of insolence, the grey eyes that surveyed the passers-by a hint of laughter, for he found life very amusing.

Of medium height and rather stockily built, he looked younger than his thirty-nine years. His pleasant face was unlined, and his smooth black hair — for he wore no hat this bright summer morning — was innocent of grey.

Throughout the length of Fleet Street he was known as 'Farry,' and was as popular among his fellow reporters as he was with the taciturn Mr. Ebbs, the gaunt news editor of the *Morning Herald*, on the staff of which enterprising paper he held the position of crime reporter since the tragic death of poor Hallam Winchester, who had drunk himself into the grave two years before.

Most people who were introduced to Farringdon Street for the first time were inclined to wonder how he got his name, but the explanation was a simple one. At the tender age of six weeks he had been found by a startled policeman on the steps of an office building wrapped in many shawls and yelling lustily. There was no clue to his parents, and sooner than let the baby go to a foundling home, the good-natured constable and his wife had adopted it.

'We'll call him Farringdon,' declared Mr. Flecker, when his wife brought up the subject of a name for the infant. 'It were in Farringdon Street that I found 'im, and Farringdon is as good a name as any.'

As Farringdon Flecker he passed through boyhood and eventually joined the police force at the wish of his foster-father, who had now attained the rank of sergeant. When that big-hearted man was killed in a fight with a drunken gang three years later, young Farringdon resigned from the city police at the urgent request of Mrs. Flecker, and to the regret of his superiors who had marked him for promotion.

He had always had a hankering for journalism, and under the pen-name of 'Farringdon Street' had contributed several articles to obscure provincial newspapers during his service as a police officer. Now he was able to devote his whole time to that precarious job, and speedily achieved success.

When Mrs. Flecker died two years after her husband, Farringdon was holding down a job as junior reporter on the staff of the *Morning Herald*. His uncanny flair for crime stories soon brought him to the notice of the news editor. It was only natural that when that erratic genius, Hallam Winchester, finally succumbed to the drink which had kept him alive for so many years, young Farringdon Street should step into his shoes. The pen-name under which he had first started to write stuck to him, and few people remembered the Flecker or were aware that he possessed any other name.

He came blithely along Fleet Street and ran up the steps of the huge building which housed the activities of the *Morning Herald*. Except for one man the reporters' room was empty, and this industrious individual, who was busily thumping a typewriter, never even looked round as Street came in.

'Hello, Curley!' said Farringdon. 'What are you doing?'

Curley Brown grunted without ceasing his onslaught on the typewriter. 'A column and a half on the opening of the new bridge,' he said. 'Nearly finished, too, thank heaven!'

Farringdon Street sprawled in a chair and searched in his pocket for a cigarette. 'What was it like?' he asked, referring to the function which had taken place that morning.

'Like every other that has ever been seen,' muttered the reporter. 'Shut up, Farry, for the Lord's sake! You've made me make two mistakes already.'

Farringdon grinned, showing his even white teeth, and took no notice of the

15

exhortation. 'A good newspaper man should be able to work under any conditions,' he admonished severely. 'It's a matter of concentration — ' He stopped and looked towards the door as it was jerked open and a shirt-sleeved sub-editor thrust in his head.

'The 'Old Man' wants you, Street,' he said, and with a sigh Farringdon got to his feet.

'What's 'broken'?' he demanded.

The shirt-sleeved man shook his head. 'I don't know,' he said. 'He's got a girl with him. A good looker, too. He told me to shoot you along as soon as you came in.'

Farringdon raised his eyebrows. 'Well, well! Wonders will never cease.' He walked along the corridor to the door of Mr. Samuel Ebbs's office, tapped, and in answer to the gruff invitation, turned the handle and entered the news editor's room.

'I've been waiting for you, Street!' snapped Mr. Ebbs, a small, bald-headed man with a thin, pale face, staring across the huge untidy desk at which he sat.

16

'What have you been doing with yourself?'

Farringdon Street said nothing. It is doubtful even if he heard the question which had been put to him. His entire attention was taken up with the third occupant of the room.

By the side of the news editor's desk sat a girl who, at first sight, looked scarcely more than a child, and Farringdon stared, for never in his life had he seen anything so lovely. The illusion of extreme youth was not dispelled by his scrutiny, but he saw that she was really older than she looked. The full red lips were firm; the blue eyes that met his had a decision of character that could not have been possessed by a person in their teens, as he had at first supposed her to be. The little hat that she wore failed to conceal the fine texture of her fair hair, and as she caught the admiration in his glance she flushed slightly.

Mr. Ebbs's thin lips twitched as he saw the impression which his visitor had created, and he grunted. 'This is Miss Lesley Thane,' he said. 'She only arrived in England yesterday afternoon.' He turned his head towards the girl. 'Miss Thane, this is Mr. Street, our crime man.'

She smiled as Farringdon acknowledged the introduction. 'How do you do?' she said, and her voice had the sweet, low quality of the well-bred college girl, with only the faintest tinge of an accent that rather added to its charm.

'Miss Thane brought a letter of introduction to the chief,' explained Mr. Ebbs, 'and he referred her to me. I don't know whether we shall be able to help her, but I want you to do all you can.'

Farringdon nodded. He was wondering what kind of help this girl was in need of.

'It's about my uncle, Mr. Street,' she said. 'I've already told Mr. Ebbs. You have probably heard of him: Felix Dexon.'

Farringdon's eyes widened. 'Felix Dexon!' he exclaimed. 'Is he your uncle? Yes, I certainly have heard of him. So has most of the world.'

Two years before, the papers had been full of Felix Dexon. An American by birth, he had come to England for a rest cure, and six months after he had reached

London had vanished from the face of the earth. But although from that time to the present no one had set eyes on him, they had heard from him. His lawyers in New York had received a letter informing them that he was away on a tour, and instructing them to draw his quarterly income from his bank and forward it to the Credit Donne, in Paris. Dexon had made a lot of money in real estate at the time of the boom, and this he had re-invested in first-class shares and securities. His income was enormous, amounting to nearly four hundred thousand a year.

For some time after his disappearance his American lawyers had transferred the quarterly payments to the Paris bank as instructed. And then, hearing nothing more from him, had got suspicious and refused to transfer any more without further instructions. Their answer came in the form of a stiff letter from Dexon telling them that if he liked to keep his whereabouts secret it was his own affair, but unless they complied with his wishes he would place his affairs in the hands of another firm. The letter was, without any doubt, in his own handwriting and bore his usual signature. The lawyers could do nothing but capitulate, and since then his income had been regularly paid to the Credit Donne in Paris.

The cheques which had been presented at this bank had been subjected to the scrutiny of a handwriting expert, whose report had been that the signatures were genuine. The cheques were nearly all made payable to self and were accompanied by a note authorising the manager to send the money under registered packet to various hotels. These letters had apparently been posted all over the world, for each postmark bore the stamp of a different country.

Nothing had ever been seen of the missing man since his disappearance from London, and the papers, after giving much prominence to the eccentricity of the wealthy American, had let the matter die down, other and more topical sensations taking its place in their columns.

Farringdon Street had been greatly interested at the time, and he regarded the slim girl before him with freshened attention. 'How do you think we can help you?' he asked.

She shook her head. 'I don't know,' she answered. 'You see, I am rather worried about Uncle Felix. I don't think he's staying away of his own accord. And neither do his lawyers. I've had interviews with them, and, like me, they're under the impression that something has happened to him. The editor the *New York Courier* is a great friend of mine, and I said I was coming to England to see if I could find anything that would throw a light on Uncle's disappearance. He suggested that I should come to the *Morning Herald*. He is a personal friend of Lord Cornfield. It's useless going to the police because they could do nothing. Scotland Yard have been cabled repeatedly, but say that there is no evidence to prove that Uncle Felix met with foul play, and that if he likes to hide himself it's his own affair.'

Mr. Ebbs grunted. 'They're quite right,' he said. 'There is no evidence. In fact, all the evidence there is seems to show that he's stopping away of his own accord. The signatures on the letters and cheques are his own.'

Again she nodded. 'I know,' she said, 'and yet I'm certain that something has happened to him.'

'What do you think has happened to him?' asked Farringdon.

She made a gesture of uncertainty. 'I don't know,' she answered. 'But I'm worried. That's why I've come over.'

Mr. Ebbs frowned. 'I don't know what we can do, Miss Thane,' he said dubiously. 'Everything that could be done was done two years ago.'

She looked a little disappointed. 'I suppose it is rather difficult,' she admitted. 'But I was wondering if — if something perhaps had been overlooked.' She hesitated. 'I mean — the police were so sure at the time that Uncle was just being eccentric, that perhaps they didn't . . . ' She stopped, at a loss how to finish the sentence.

'Put all their energy into it?' suggested Farringdon, and she gave him a grateful look. 'You may be near the mark there, Miss Thane. I suppose you've nothing definite as a basis for your belief that something has happened to your uncle?'

She shook her head. 'No. It's only just an idea of mine,' she replied.

Farringdon looked at Mr. Ebbs, and the news editor frowned. The note that had reached him that morning from Lord Cornfield had been very emphatic. The *Morning Herald's* proprietor's instructions were that every assistance was to be given to Miss Lesley Thane, and that letter lay on the desk in front of him.

'You're not on anything at the moment, are you?' he grunted.

Farringdon shook his head.

'Well, you'd better look into this business,' went on the news editor grudgingly. 'If there's anything in it it'll make a first-class story.' His tone rather suggested that, privately, he thought there was nothing in it.

'I'm sure there's something in it,' said the girl quietly. 'I can't tell you why I am so sure, but I just feel that Uncle Felix is not staying away of his own accord.'

'Do you mean you think he's been kidnapped?' asked Farringdon.

She shrugged her shoulders helplessly.

'I don't know what I think,' she said.

Mr. Ebbs fidgeted with the papers on his desk, and Farringdon could see that he was anxious to end the interview. 'Suppose we go and have some coffee and talk it over?' he suggested to the girl, and when she accepted, the news editor's melancholy face visibly brightened

'That's a good idea,' he said, almost heartily, 'and if you can hit on anything, Street, I don't mind telling you that it's the scoop of your life.' He rose to his feet as the girl held out her hand.

'I'm very pleased to have met you, Miss Thane, and we'll do all we can to help you.'

She thanked him, and Farringdon escorted her to the door.

'Come in and see me at three o'clock, Street,' called Mr. Ebbs as they crossed the threshold, and he promptly immersed himself in the mass of work awaiting his attention, forgetting in less than five minutes that such a person as Lesley Thane existed.

'This isn't going to be an easy job you've taken on, Miss Thane,' said Farringdon when they were seated opposite each other at a secluded table in a café in Fleet Street.

'I know it isn't,' she answered, 'but I feel that something ought to be done. The police won't do anything more than they have, and since I am Uncle Felix's only relative it's up to me to do it. That's why I've come to England. You see, Mr. Street,' she went on when the waitress had taken their order, 'he was more like a father to me than an uncle, and one of the things that makes me so sure that something has happened to him is the fact that he hasn't written. The only people who have had any communication from him since he disappeared are his lawyers and the bank. If he was really on a world tour he would have written to me.'

Farringdon pulled out a cigarette-case and lighted a cigarette. 'What sort of man was he?' he asked.

'He was a dear,' she replied instantly. 'I don't think he had an enemy in the world. I'll have a cigarette, too, if you don't mind.'

'I'm sorry,' he apologised, and offered her his case. She helped herself and blew a cloud of smoke across the table.

'I don't mind telling you, Miss Thane,' he said, 'that quite apart from helping you, I'm interested. I always thought there was something peculiar about Dexon's disappearance. Had he any intimate friends in England?'

She wrinkled her forehead. 'I only know of one,' she said after a moment's thought. 'Mr. Clifford Feldon. I don't know where he lives, though.'

He pulled out an envelope and jotted down the name. 'It shouldn't be difficult to find him,' he said. 'I'll have inquiries made at once. You see, what we've got to do is try and trace your uncle's movements up to the time he disappeared. I don't know how far the police went regarding that, but I've got a good friend at Scotland Yard and I'll ask him. When we've found the last place he was seen at we can begin from there. Of course, the fact that he vanished two years ago is going to make it difficult.'

'I know,' she said despondently. 'It seems almost a hopeless task.'

'Oh, it's by no means hopeless,' said

Farringdon cheerily, 'but I think it's going to take time. I'll read up on all the back files relating to his disappearance and see if they supply any information that will help.'

He put several more questions concerning Felix Dexon's private life, secured a list of his friends in America, and then as the girl, with a glance at her watch, said she must go: 'Where are you staying, in case I should wish to communicate with you?' he asked.

'How silly of me, I nearly forgot to tell you,' she laughed. 'I'm staying at the Regent. It's in Berkeley Street, I think.'

'I know it quite well,' said Farringdon. He beckoned to the waitress for the bill.

'You don't know how grateful I am,' she said as they passed out into the street.

'It's awfully good of you to help me.'

'It's nothing of the sort,' he retorted. 'It's my job. If you're right and we can discover what's happened to Dexon, the *Morning Herald* will have the laugh of every other paper in Fleet Street.'

At her request he hailed a passing cab, and it drew into the kerb. Crossing the strip of pavement, he helped the girl in and gave the driver the address of her hotel. She smiled him a farewell as the taxi moved away, and he stood looking after it.

A few doors away, a long black saloon was standing by the sidewalk, and no sooner had the taxi containing Lesley Thane pulled away than it began to move slowly, and though it was obviously a powerful machine it made no effort to overtake the cab.

Farringdon watched it thoughtfully, and then, acting on a sudden impulse, he snapped his fingers at another empty taxi that came into view, and jerked open the door as it slowed down at his signal.

'Don't stop!' he snapped at the astonished driver. 'Follow that big black saloon in front.'

'All right, mate,' said the taxi-man, and the reporter sprang in and slammed the door. He had come to his decision on the spur of the moment, and was wondering whether or not his sudden instinct was going to lead him on a wild goose chase.

He soon found that he was right. The big black saloon was trailing the cab containing Lesley Thane. Keeping a few yards behind, it twined in and out of the traffic and, negotiating a maze of side turnings, eventually stopped as the girl's taxi drew up outside her hotel.

Farringdon stopped his cab too and, paying the driver, got out and crossed the road rapidly in the direction of the machine. At least, he thought, he would have a good look at the occupants, but as he got near the big car shot forward.

He was in the middle of the road and he sprang aside as the long radiator swerved towards him, and he was only just in time. As it was, the right wing ripped a strip of cloth from his jacket and sent him staggering backwards. When he recovered his balance the back of the saloon was disappearing down a side turning.

Farringdon looked after it and his mouth was set. The action had been a deliberate attempt to injure him — perhaps kill him. The owner of the black car, who took such an interest in Lesley Thane's movements, evidently objected to his interference.

Turning back, he saw the white-faced

girl staring at him from the portico of the hotel. 'Mr. Street!' she gasped. 'How did you get here? You did give me a scare. I thought you'd been run over.'

'I believe that was the intention,' replied the reporter grimly.

She looked at him in astonishment. 'Do you mean it wasn't accidental?' she exclaimed.

'That is exactly what I do mean,' he said. 'That car followed you from Fleet Street this morning.'

'Followed me?' she repeated.

He nodded. 'Yes — somebody is very interested in your movements.'

'Then I was right,' she cried suddenly.

'What do you mean?' he demanded.

'I didn't say anything before,' she replied, 'because I thought it was just imagination or nerves, or something like that, but I've had a feeling ever since I landed at Southampton that I was being watched.'

'Have you seen anyone following you?' asked Farringdon quickly.

'No. Only just a feeling,' she answered. 'Who can it be?'

'That's an easy one to answer,' said the

reporter. 'If there is anything fishy in your uncle's disappearance, the people responsible have got the wind up at your presence in England. I've got the number of the car but I expect it's a fake.' He looked down ruefully at his torn coat. 'I must be getting back to the office,' he went on, 'but before I go I think I ought to warn you to be careful. Don't go out after dark, and even in the daytime keep in the more populated streets.'

Her eyes widened. 'Do you think I'm in any danger?'

He had no wish to frighten her, but it was just as well that she should be on her guard. 'I don't know,' he replied. 'But be careful.' He bade her goodbye and went towards Piccadilly, looking for a taxi, and as he drove back to Fleet Street his brows were drawn together in a frown.

The incident of the black saloon had been impressive, and it could only mean one thing: Lesley Thane's vague forebodings concerning her uncle's disappearance had been correct, and the people responsible were taking the precaution of trying to prevent the inquiry being re-opened.

3

The Man in the Night

Lesley Thane sat before the open window of her bedroom, looking out over the tops of the adjoining buildings at the glow in the sky that marked Piccadilly Circus. The night was very still, save for the distant rumble of the traffic, and the air was oppressive She had already undressed but never felt less like sleep in her life, and therefore, slipping on a light dressing-gown, she had seated herself by the window hoping that the air would make her feel drowsy.

She turned over in her mind her interview of the morning, and concluded that she had started well. She liked Farringdon Street. There was something very human and very kindly about him. She was impressed by the suggestion of his capability, the latent strength in him, and felt that she could not have put the matter of her uncle's disappearance into better hands.

Nevertheless, there was cause for the vague uneasiness that refused to leave her.

Who had followed her? Who was sufficiently interested in her movements to shadow her? Perhaps the reporter had been mistaken about the car. The near accident might really have been carelessness on the part of the driver; the fact of the car following her taxi just coincidence or capable of some simple explanation.

She tried to bolster up her courage by trying to believe this, but failed. She was very wide awake, although the hour was late, and presently, turning on the light with a sigh, she picked up the evening newspaper which had been brought to her room and glanced through it. But she found nothing to interest her, and presently turned her attention to the novel she had been reading earlier in the evening.

Locking the door, she took off the dressing gown and got into bed. For an hour she tried to concentrate her mind upon the story, and a church clock was striking one when she finally gave up the attempt and, putting the book on the bedside table, switched out the light and composed herself for sleep.

The half-hour struck, then two, then she must have dozed. Hazily in her sleep she heard three chime, and was suddenly wide awake, but it was not the sound of the clock striking that had awakened her; it was the consciousness of danger. She sat up in, bed and listened, but could hear nothing. Farringdon Street's warning of the morning came to her mind, and for no reason at all she felt filled with terror. And then she heard something.

A sound of heavy, irregular breathing. It came from the window. Paralysed with fear, she stared with wide eyes at the blue-black square. As she looked, the horrible thing came into view. She saw a hand reach up out of the darkness and grip the window-sill, and while she sat with dry throat and shaking limbs a head appeared — a shapeless black blot, the face swathed in some sort of hood.

She tried to scream, but the vocal cords in her throat seemed dried up and useless.

The next instant the intruder was in the room. He moved stealthily towards the bed in a half-crouching position, so that silhouetted against the patch of night sky visible through the window he looked like some deformed shape conjured up in a nightmare. He stretched out a long, lean hand and began to feel carefully over the bed, and then suddenly Lesley found her voice and screamed.

The masked intruder uttered a muffled oath, and her second scream was strangled at its birth by the fingers which gripped her neck. But her fear lent her strength and she beat off this clutching hand and sprang from the bed.

In the dim light of the lightening sky she saw her assailant fumbling beneath the long black coat he wore, and then caught the gleam of the thin-bladed knife that he drew from his pocket.

She screamed again as he advanced towards her, and then he had caught her by the shoulders and the knife was raised to strike. And at that moment there came a rush of feet up the corridor outside and somebody thumped on the door.

'What's the matter in there?' cried a voice. 'Open this door!'

There was the sound of a body being

hurled against the panels and the door shivered and cracked.

With an exclamation of alarm the night intruder swung round, and dropping his knife, ran for the window. Lesley fell back against the wall breathless, her heart thumping painfully, and then with a crash that sounded like an earthquake the door burst open.

'Miss Thane, are you all right?' cried an anxious voice from the threshold, and her relief was so great that she nearly fainted.

It was Farringdon Street!

'Yes, he's gone,' she managed to gasp out, and the reporter felt for the switch and pressed it on.

As the room became flooded with light, she saw that he was fully dressed. 'What happened?' he asked rapidly before she could ask the question that hovered on her lips, and he uttered a silent whistle when she told him. 'Gosh! I was only just in time,' he said. 'I was afraid something like this might happen.'

She looked at him in questioning amazement.

'I booked the room next to yours this

afternoon,' he said, answering the un-spoken question, and then going over to the window he looked down. 'Oh, yes!' he said softly, and drew in his head. 'There's an iron fire-escape to all the rooms. That's the way the fellow came and went. There's no sign of him, though. He's a quick mover, I'll say that.'

'Did you expect — ' She left the sentence unfinished and he nodded.

'I thought something might happen,' he replied, 'and I thought it would be as well if I was on the spot. I didn't say anything to you in case you would be scared.'

'Well, I'm very glad you were here,' she said, and suddenly realising the scantiness of her attire, flushed and hurriedly pulled on her dressing gown.

Farringdon carefully picked up the long-bladed knife with his handkerchief and slipped it into his pocket.

'This may prove interesting,' he said. 'Now I think I'll be going, Miss Thane. I don't expect you'll be troubled any more tonight.'

'Thank you,' she said. 'I'm very grateful to you. I don't know what I should have done if you hadn't been here.'

He thought of the weapon in his breast pocket and had no doubt of the result.

As he went into the corridor he saw the partially dressed and agitated manager coming hastily towards the room. 'What's been happening? What's the trouble?' he inquired excitedly. 'People have been complaining of the noise up here. What's it all about?'

Farringdon took him gently by the arm. 'I broke down a door,' he explained. 'Somebody tried to get into Miss Thane's room by the window.'

The manager eyed him suspiciously. 'Why are you dressed?' he demanded. 'And why should you take it upon yourself to break open the door? If there was any trouble *I* should have been informed. All this is likely to damage the reputation of the hotel.'

'A murder would have damaged the reputation of the hotel far more!' snapped Farringdon. 'And that's what would have happened if I had waited to wake you up.'

'A murder!' squeaked the man. 'I don't understand — '

'There's quite a lot you don't understand,' broke in the reporter, 'and I'm not going to explain standing about in the passage. If you'll come into my room I'll tell you all about it.'

He dragged the protesting manager away and in the privacy of his bedroom told him all about it, and told him to such purpose that it was a very chastened man who eventually wished him good night and went back to his disturbed slumbers.

Before undressing Farringdon took out the dagger and locked it in his suitcase, and he could not repress the slight shudder that passed over him as he pictured what might have happened if his foresight had not led him to take precautions.

4

Clifford Feldon's Address

Farringdon Street left the Regent Hotel early on the following morning and arrived in Fleet Street just as Mr. Ebbs was preparing to start the day's work. The news editor listened with interest to his account of the previous night's happenings.

'Looks as if there was something in this business of Dexon's disappearance,' he remarked. 'You'd better look after that girl, Street. She ought to leave the hotel where she's staying and go somewhere safer.' He rubbed his thin hands together happily and Farringdon looked at him disparagingly.

'I believe you're sorry that nothing did happen to her!' he accused.

'Well, it would have made a grand story,' said Mr. Ebbs. 'Niece of vanished millionaire stabbed in hotel room!'

Farriagdon sniffed. 'You're inhuman, Ebbs,' he said. 'I believe you'd cheerfully see your own mother killed for the sake of a story.'

Mr. Ebbs treated the remark as a compliment. 'I'm a newspaper man first and a human being afterwards,' he answered. 'You can't be both and be successful. Still, she's a nice girl and I wouldn't like to see anything happen to her, so you'd better get her out that hotel as quickly as possible.'

'I'm thinking the same,' said Farringdon. 'I wonder if Williams could take her?'

'Who's Williams?' grunted the news editor.

'He used to be a policeman,' answered Farringdon, 'but he's retired now. He's got a boarding-house in Bloomsbury somewhere, and she'd be safer there than anywhere. I'll get on the phone.' He looked up the number in the directory and put the call through.

'I'll look after her, Mr. Street,' said Williams when he explained. 'I'll bet no one'll get at her while she's staying with me, though I wouldn't mind if they had try. I could do with a good old scrap. It'd be like old times.'

'You might get more than you bargained for, Williams, with these people,' said the reporter. 'Apparently they fight with cold steel.'

'I'd take a chance on that,' replied the ex-policeman. 'You send the young lady along, Mr. Street, and my missus'll make her comfortable, and I'll see that she don't come to no harm.'

Farringdon arranged that the girl should be round at midday and hung up the receiver. He reported the conversation to Mr. Ebbs, and the news editor grunted. 'You can spend all your time on this business, Street,' he said. 'I believe there's a big story in it. Go all out for it and we won't argue the expense sheet.'

Farringdon grinned and left the office. He had spent the whole of the previous day reading up everything that was known of Felix Dexon, and at the end had been forced to admit that it was very little.

The millionaire had walked out of the Ritz-Carlton one morning and never returned. Later had come a letter containing money for his bill and instructions to forward his luggage to the cloakroom at Victoria

Station to be called for. There had been no word of explanation for his sudden departure, and from that day to the present he had vanished into obscurity.

Farringdon had searched the London directory for the address of Mr. Clifford Feldon but had failed to find him in that voluminous tome. A call to his friend at Scotland Yard, however, had resulted in a promise to have Mr. Feldon's whereabouts looked up. The reporter had also, as a forlorn hope, got on to the registration department of the County Hall, but as he had expected, the number of the car that had nearly run him down was unknown.

Leaving the offices of the *Morning Herald*, he went back to the Regent to find Lesley Thane at breakfast. To her he outlined the arrangements he had made with Williams, the ex-policeman, and after a great deal of argument she reluctantly consented to fall in with his wishes.

After he had escorted her to the boarding-house in Bloomsbury he set off for the Ritz-Carlton, and a few seconds after his arrival at that magnificent hotel, where they charge you for walking across the lounge, he was closeted with the manager.

Monsieur Rimell shook his glistening head when he heard what Farringdon required. 'I can give you no other information than I gave the newspaper men at the time,' he said. 'Monsieur Dexon just left one morning, that's all.'

'Did he have many friends while he was staying here?' inquired Farringdon.

The manager shrugged his fat shoulders. 'Oh, yes, many,' he replied. 'But I do not remember their names, except one: Monsieur Feldon. He came once, twice, several times.'

'What was this Feldon like?' asked the reporter, and he received only the vaguest description. It would have fit at least half the men who walked down Piccadilly to their clubs. He tried everything he could think of to get the manager to add to his meagre stock of information, but at the end of an hour had drawn a blank.

From the Ritz-Carlton he went to Victoria and interviewed the station-master. That official remembered the luggage belonging to Felix Dexon. Was he ever likely to forget it? For weeks he had been besieged, and so had the porters in charge of the 'left luggage' department. It had only been there a few hours and then it had been fetched away in a car. He didn't know who had fetched it away. He had never seen them. Perhaps the porter who had looked after it could help there, though the station-master was very doubtful. Long training in the service of the railway company had made him very doubtful about everything. Yes, the same porter was still there; in fact he was just going off duty. If Farringdon wanted to catch him he'd have to hurry. The station-master nodded good morning with every evidence of relief, and the reporter went round to the 'left luggage' office.

The porter he wanted to see was just going. Farringdon, after explaining who he was and what he wanted, suggested an adjournment to the buffet, a suggestion that was accepted with alacrity.

'You've no idea what a lot of free beer I got out of that luggage,' said the porter, whose name was Smith, draining the foaming contents of the glass in two gulps, 'and now I'm getting more.'

Farringdon took the hint and the glass was refilled.

'I couldn't rightly tell you what the bloke was like,' confided Mr. Smith, having made sure of two beers and got halfway through the third. 'I didn't see mud of 'is face. 'e wore a big brimmed 'at, though,' he added helpfully, 'an' 'e was tall and stoutish.'

That was all Mr. Smith could offer in the way of information, and Farringdon left the station concluding that his morning's work so far had been practically wasted. He had one more call to make, however, and Inspector Hallick stretched a lean hand across his bare desk as the reporter was shown into his office at Scotland Yard.

'Sit down, Street,' he said. 'What's all this about Felix Dexon? You only told me a bit over the phone.'

Farringdon told him some more, and the lean man rubbed his grizzled hair. 'Damn queer,' he grunted. 'We were always of the opinion there was something fishy at the bottom of his disappearance, but of course we couldn't move because there was no evidence to show that he hadn't gone away voluntarily. We made one or two inquiries and then the matter was dropped. The police are pretty chary, as you know, of interfering in people's private business, and Felix Dexon might very easily have had good reasons for vanishing as he did.' He hunted among the papers on his desk and produced an oblong slip. 'I've got that address you wanted — Clifford Feldon's, you know,' he went on. 'Here you are. 'Clifford Feldon, Silverleaves, Deneswood Valley Estate'.'

Farringdon Street took the paper from his hand and frowned. 'Isn't that the place where that fellow was murdered a fortnight ago?' he asked.

Hallick nodded. 'That's right,' he said. 'A man was killed there. An habitual criminal called Lew Miller. There's a bit of a mystery about that. He'd only recently been released from prison after serving a seven-year stretch for burglary and being found in possession of firearms. Mr. Blessington, the builder of the estate, saw him the day before, and apparently Miller was looking for a fellow called Sam Gates, but he must have come to the wrong place, for nobody had ever heard the name round Deneswood.'

Farringdon Street listened, but he only heard a word here and there, for he was wondering. Deneswood Valley was the home of Clifford Feldon, the man who had been a constant visitor at Felix Dexon's hotel just before his appearance. Was there any connection between this disappearance and the murder of Lew Miller? And if so, did Clifford Feldon know more about both than he ought to?

5

The Man Who Was Drunk

Farringdon Street came to Deneswood Valley in the dusk of the evening, and he had to admit, as he stopped his disreputable car at the end of the road and took stock of the estate, that he had seldom looked upon a scene of such quiet beauty.

The place seemed to breathe the very spirit of peace, and yet, amid this pleasant environment, he remembered, one murder had already been committed, and in these sylvan surroundings lived a man who might very well hold the secret of it, and of the disappearance of Felix Dexon.

The drive gates of the various houses came out onto a broad gravel path that enclosed the central garden on three sides, and Farringdon was just getting out of his car to look round for 'Silverleaves', Mr. Clifford Feldon's residence, when a man came into view round a clump of shrubbery.

He was a big man, pompous-looking, and walked with a leisurely step as though conscious of his dignity. As he caught sight of Farringdon he eyed him gravely and would have passed if the reporter had not addressed him.

'Good evening,' he said pleasantly. 'I am looking for the house of Mr. Clifford Feldon. Perhaps you can help me?'

'Most certainly I can,' said the other, his placid face breaking into a sedate smile. 'That is Mr. Feldon's house.' He pointed. 'The second gateway before you come to the turn.'

Farringdon thanked him. 'This is a very beautiful locality,' he said, and the big man positively beamed.

'I am glad you like it,' he said heartily. 'You could not have paid me a greater compliment, since I, to a large extent, am responsible for its being.'

'Then you are Mr. Blessington,' said the reporter, and he looked at the other with renewed interest.

Mr. Blessington inclined his head. 'I had no idea that I was so famous,' he said modestly.

'I remembered reading an account of your activities with regard to the Deneswood estate when that unfortunate tramp was killed here,' said Farringdon, and Mr. Blessington's placid face clouded.

'A most unfortunate occurrence,' he said, shaking his head solemnly. 'A terrible thing. It brought our little estate into prominence and gave it a lot of unwelcome publicity.' He looked curiously at the reporter, and then after a short pause: 'I seem to recognise you, sir. Have we by any chance met before?'

Farringdon shook his head. 'I don't think so. My name is Street, Farringdon Street.'

Mr. Blessington frowned for a moment in a puzzled way, and then his face cleared. 'Of course.' He nodded slowly. 'I have seen your photograph in the *Morning Herald*. An admirable paper. That was what made me feel I had met you before. I remember reading your account of the Lambert case.' He stopped and hesitated. 'May I ask if you — er — if you are here professionally? In connection, perhaps, with, the murder?'

'You may certainly ask,' replied Farringdon,

'and I can assure you with truth that I am not here in connection with the murder.' He did not add the reason for his visit, though Mr. Blessington was obviously waiting for him to do so.

'That is a great relief to me,' he remarked with a sigh as Farringdon remained silent. 'For the moment I thought that horrible business was going to be re-opened. To a sensitive man like myself, Mr. Street, the inquest and cross-examination by the police was exquisite torture.'

'It must have been very unpleasant for you,' murmured reporter without much sympathy.

'Well, I mustn't detain you with my gossip,' said Mr. Blessington, noticing the slight movement the other made towards his car. 'Perhaps you will come back some day let me show you round.'

'I should be delighted,' said Farringdon as he climbed into the driving seat, and Mr. Blessington bowed and stood looking after him as he sent the car along the gravel road and disappeared through the drive gates of Mr. Clifford Feldon's house.

It was a respectably sized, heavily timbered house of pseudo-Elizabethan architecture, nestling amid thickly clustering trees. The flowerbeds were gay with colour, and closely shaven lawns were as smooth as a billiard table.

A trim maid in cool grey and white came in answer to Farringdon's ring and disappeared with the card he handed to her. After an interval she returned. 'Will you come this way, sir?' she said, and led him across a wide hall and ushered him into a room on the right. 'Mr. Feldon will join you in a moment.' She went away, closing the door behind her, and Farringdon glanced about him.

In some respects the room was remarkable. It was long, and because of its length seemed narrower than it was, and an enormous window at one end looked out onto the garden. In the centre was a large, carved oak fireplace, obviously of great age, which he concluded had evidently been purchased at some sale and fitted into the house. The walls were panelled in oak, and he noticed at once the most complete absence of books, which was peculiar in room that was obviously used as a study.

Evidently Mr. Feldon was not a literary man, and made no attempt to deceive the casual caller that he was. The pictures on the walls were mostly etchings, and quite valuable. The furniture was good and modern. Two deep settees, one by the window and one by the fireplace; a large, flat-topped desk; several comfortable easy chairs; and a very beautifully carved cabinet of Eastern design constituted the bulk. Everything was of the best, and Farringdon decided that Mr. Feldon was not lacking in wealth.

He turned from his contemplation of the garden as the door opened and a man came in. He was thin and gaunt, with a shock of iron-grey hair that no amount of brushing seemed to master. He looked at the reporter from a pair of sunken eyes that were like pieces of black jet set in alabaster, so white vas his face. As he advanced, his gait was unsteady and his hands trembled violently.

Farringdon's sudden suspicion was confirmed when he spoke. Mr. Clifford

Feldon had been drinking, and was within measurable distance of being drunk.

'What do you want with me?' he asked thickly. 'We've had no peace since the murder. The place has been overrun with you reporters.'

'I wish to have a few words with you concerning Mr. Felix Dexon,' said Farringdon, and the result of his words was extraordinary. The man's white face went a dirty grey and he staggered slightly.

'I don't know anything about him!' he cried. 'Why do you come and worry me? Why should I know anything?'

'I understand that you are one of his greatest friends,' said the reporter, 'and as I want some information regarding Mr. Dexon I naturally came to you.'

'I can give you no information,' said Mr. Feldon with an irritable gesture.

The man's nerves were in a pretty bad way, thought Farringdon. There was a lurking fear in every movement, and drink had not done anything to help matters. He kept on throwing nervous glances over his shoulder as though he expected somebody else to come into the room.

There was no doubt about it — Mr. Clifford Feldon was frightened, and badly frightened at that. The question was, what had scared him? Farringdon's visit, or something else?

'Why should you think I could tell you anything about Dexon?' he went on, mastering his emotions by a prodigious effort. 'He's gone away, hasn't he? I haven't seen him for over two years.'

'I'm not saying that you have, Mr. Feldon,' said Farringdon smoothly. 'But you were with him, I believe, just before he disappeared.'

'Who told you that?' shouted Clifford Feldon. 'I never saw him on the day he disappeared. And anyway, what's it got to do with you? What's it got to do with anybody? He went away of his own accord, didn't he?'

'That is a question I can't answer,' replied the reporter, eyeing the man steadily. 'And it is for that very purpose I've come to see you. Did Felix Dexon disappear of his own accord?'

Feldon stared at him, and then passed the tip of his tongue over his dry lips. 'I don't know what you mean,' he muttered hoarsely.

Farringdon decided on a bold stroke. In the man's present condition it might have some effect. 'This is what I mean,' he said, speaking slowly and deliberately. 'There is every reason to believe that Felix Dexon is being held prisoner somewhere, most probably somewhere in this neighbourhood.'

His words certainly achieved an effect — an electrical effect. Clifford Feldon went limp like a pricked balloon, and had to grip the edge of the desk for support. 'It's a lie!' he choked. 'A lie! Dexon went away of own accord, I tell you. Why bring all this up again? The inquiry was dropped.' He broke off abruptly and glanced uneasily about him. 'I'm not well,' he mumbled, lowering his trembling limbs into a chair. 'I've had a lot of worry lately.'

'The greatest of your worries could be removed if you were to tell me what you know concerning Felix Dexon,' aid Farringdon

'I know nothing,' stammered Feldon.

'Why do you keep pestering me? Why don't you leave me alone?'

The reporter shrugged his shoulders. 'Perhaps you would prefer the police to question you?' he suggested. It was sheer bluff, but it had the effect he desired. The man started half out of his chair.

'No, no, no!' he almost screamed. 'Oh, God! Am I never going to have any peace?'

'Mr. Feldon,' said Farringdon a little more gently, 'it's useless denying that you know anything. You're giving yourself away by every word and action. Why not tell me the truth?'

Feldon raised his haggard face and stared at his questioner. 'If only I dared,' he whispered. And then: 'No, no! I don't know what I'm saying. Take no notice of me. I don't know what I'm saying.' He glanced round him again suspiciously, as though fearful of a possible eavesdropper.

'You're afraid of someone,' said Farringdon suddenly. 'Who?'

'I'm not afraid of anybody. I'm ill, that's all. Why don't you go and leave me alone?'

'You're ill because you're frightened,' retorted the reporter, 'and because you've been trying to bolster up your courage with drink. Come, Mr. Feldon, will you tell me all that you know, or must I go and tell the police what I suspect?' He was taking a risk and he knew it. If Feldon was an innocent man, he could make it very unpleasant indeed for Farringdon.

There was a long silence, so long that the reporter was on the point of breaking it when Feldon spoke. 'Supposing,' he said hesitantly, 'a man had been forced into doing something — something criminal — because he couldn't help it; because the — person who made him do it knew something about him and held that something over his head? What would be his position with regard to the law?'

'You mean if he'd been blackmailed into a criminal act against his will?' said Farringdon.

The other nodded.

'The law would undoubtedly take into account the circumstances, particularly if the man you mentioned did all in his power to help by telling all he knew.'

There was another pause.

'Mr. Street,' — Feldon leaned forward eagerly — 'I am the man I was speaking about. For over four years I have been at the mercy of a scoundrel who has bled me consistently and forced me to do his bidding. Perhaps you can help me. You are not connected with the police.'

'What is this man's name?' asked Farringdon quickly.

'His name — ' began Feldon, and then he sat up with a jerk. 'What was that?' he cried shrilly.

'I heard nothing,' answered the reporter.

'There was a noise — over there.' The grey-haired man looked apprehensively towards the window. 'Yes, there it is again — there's somebody outside the window!'

'It's only your imagination,' said Farringdon, and going over he looked out into the garden. There was neither sight nor sound of anyone. 'There's nobody there.'

Feldon was shaking like a leaf, his face ashen.

'You were going to tell me the name of — ' began the reporter, but the other shook his head.

'I can't tell you here,' he whispered frantically, 'but I will tell you — I'll tell you everything. I can't go on like this. It's killing me. I'll tell you tonight. Do you know this place?'

'No,' answered Farringdon. 'This is the first time I've been here.'

'Well,' — Feldon spoke rapidly and jerkily — 'there's a golf course — goes down the valley — the first tee is over in the corner of the central garden. You can't miss it. I'll meet you there — at twelve o'clock tonight.'

'Why not now?' urged the reporter, who was afraid that in the interval the man might change his mind.

'No, no! There are eyes and ears watching and listening everywhere,' said the other nervously. 'You're afraid I'll change my mind? You needn't be. I'll be there, and I'll tell you everything.' He stared at the window. 'What do you think of this place, eh? Beautiful, isn't it? A paradise. A fairyland.'

'It certainly is very lovely,' answered Farringdon, rather surprised at the sudden change of subject. 'Very lovely — '

'Yes, that's what everybody thinks, except the people who live here.' Feldon laughed mirthlessly. 'Shall I tell you what it is? It's hell! It's hell! A festering sore masked in loveliness. A valley of doom. There's more devilish work going on here than you'll find in all the backstreets of Limehouse and Soho and Deptford, and I know them all. Here the very souls of men are tortured and sent to perdition.' He laughed again harshly. 'You think I'm exaggerating? Wait till after you've heard what I've got to say tonight. The Deneswood Valley Estate! The personification of all that's lovely and peaceful and beautiful! A sink of iniquity, Mr. Street! A valley of the doomed!'

He would say no more in spite of all the reporter's persuasion, and shortly afterward Farringdon took his leave. And as he drove away down the private road, the peaceful beauty of the evening and the sylvan surroundings assumed a sinister aspect.

It was queer, he told himself. But he had achieved something. Clifford Feldon did know the secret of Felix Dexon's disappearance, and that secret was also closely connected with the beautiful estate he had just left bathed in the orange light of the setting sun.

6

Death Stalks the Valley

Farringdon did not go back to London, although there would have been time. He put through a call to the *Morning Herald* offices and just caught Mr. Ebbs as he was leaving for home. The news editor listened interestedly to what he had to say and grunted his approval.

'Carry on,' he said tersely. 'You seem to have struck something.'

Farringdon filled in his time while he waited for the hour of his appointment with Feldon at a pleasant hotel near Deneswood Valley, where he was provided with an excellent dinner, and during the meal his mind was fully occupied.

So far he had cause to congratulate himself on the progress he had made, and after he had had his talk with Feldon he expected that everything would be made clear. He frowned as he remembered the

64

man's outburst just before he had left. What had he meant by referring to Deneswood as a valley of doom? Was it in connection with the fate of Felix Dexon, his own unhappy participation in that affair, or something else of which Farringdon was unaware? The reporter fancied that it was this last. Feldon had suggested that his description applied to the other residents as well as himself, but this seemed, on the face of it, absurd. If they were unhappy and hated the place so, why did they stop there? It was a free country and people could live where they liked. There was certainly nothing either unhappy or suggestive of care about the fat Mr. Blessington. The only thing that worried him was the fact that somebody had been killed on his estate.

Farringdon's eyes narrowed. That was a funny business too, the murder of Lew Miller. It had never been discovered who had killed him, or why. Could it have any connection with Felix Dexon's disappearance and Feldon? According to Mr. Blessington's evidence at the inquest, Miller had been looking for somebody and swore he lived in Deneswood, a man called Sam Gates. It seemed impossible that Miller's murder could have any bearing on Dexon's disappearance, and yet there was a possibility that it might. It least it would be worthwhile looking into. Perhaps Feldon would know something about that too. At any rate it certainly rather bore out the wild statement that Feldon had made that there was some sinister influence at work amid the peace of that beautiful place.

Well, whatever the secret of Deneswood was, he would know more about it after he had kept his appointment.

He had booked a room for the night at the hotel, and shortly after eleven-thirty he left the lounge and strolled towards the private road leading to Deneswood Estate. It was no very great distance away and he reckoned that he would just get to the tee in time.

The night was clear and the moon riding high. He paused at the beginning of the rural community, absorbing the delicate beauty of the scene. Somewhere away to his left a gramophone or wireless was playing the latest fox-trot, and the faint strains of the music mingled with the song of the nightingale from the tree-clad slopes of the hills. Here and there patches of oblong light shone out from the thick foliage, testifying to the fact that many of the residents were still wakeful. Evidently the colony did not keep country times.

Farringdon crossed the green leisurely, a smooth carpet of dove-grey in the light of the moon. Once he thought he saw a figure moving in the shadow of the bordering bushes, but concluded after a long scrutiny that his imagination was playing tricks with him.

It was curious, but as he walked across the central gardens he could feel, instead of the peacefulness which such a night should have inspired, a curious sense of unrest. He concluded that it was the subconscious effect of Feldon's words, but he could not shake it off.

He saw the streak of scarlet that marked the tee — or, to be more correct, the eighteenth hole, for the course doubled back on itself — and changed his direction.

He arrived punctually at the place Feldon had chosen, for a distant clock struck twelve as he drew level with the sandbox. The world was a place of misty hues, and from here he could look down the valley and see where the light of the moon caught a great white patch on the side of a hill in the distance. He wondered what it was, and then it came to him. It marked the side of an old quarry or gravel pit.

There was no sign of Feldon. From where he stood, Farringdon could just distinguish the dark opening of the drive that led up to his house, but there was no sign of the man himself.

A quarter of an hour went by, and the reporter began to wonder whether, after all, Feldon had changed his mind. It would be annoying if he had. It would mean —

The peaceful silence of the night was broken by a scream — a scream of terror that died abruptly.

Farringdon swung round. The cry had come from the direction of Feldon's house, and the next instant he was plunging across the grass towards the dark shadow of the drive. As he ran he heard the sound of the music stop abruptly, and coming to the gravelled walk he became aware of an excited murmur of voices near and far. The terrible scream had evidently been heard by the other residents.

Halfway up Feldon's drive he heard the sound of running steps and almost cannoned into a man who was hurrying towards him. Shooting out a hand, he gripped the newcomer by the arm.

'Here, steady, not so fast!' he cried. 'Where are you going to?'

The man gave a gasp of fear. 'Who are you' he grunted. 'Here, let go! I'm going to get help.'

'What's the matter?' asked Farringdon, without releasing his hold.

'Mr. Feldon,' whispered the man. 'He's dead! Shot!'

'Shot?' Farringdon's jaw set. 'Who are you? One of the servants?'

'Yes,' stammered the other. 'I'm going to get help.'

'You can take me up to the house first,' said Farringdon grimly. 'I'm a newspaper man.'

The servant began a faint protest, but Farringdon, still keeping hold of his arm, dragged him along in the direction of the house. He had no intention of letting go until the man had proved that he was one of the servants.

'What were you running for?' he demanded. 'Why didn't you phone for help?'

'The butler did try, sir,' answered the frightened man, 'but the telephone wouldn't work.'

'I see,' muttered Farringdon

They had reached the open door of the house and a thin man in dishevelled attire met them on the step. 'Hello!' You've been quick,' he said, and then catching sight of Farringdon's face he added sharply: 'Who's this?'

'My name is Street,' said the reporter. 'I'm on the *Morning Herald*. What has happened to Mr. Feldon?'

'He's been killed — shot, I think,' said the thin man in an altered voice. 'Didn't you call and see him this afternoon, sir?'

The reporter nodded. 'Yes, and I was to have seen him tonight,' he answered shortly. 'Where is he?'

'In his study,' answered the other.

'Then take me there at once.'

The thin man, whom Farringdon placed as the butler, turned back to the hall and led the way to the long room. The door was open and Farringdon walked in. All the lights were on and at first sight the room appeared empty, and then he saw its owner.

He lay at the other end of the room by the window, his face contorted into an expression of fear. He had been shot at close quarters, for there was a blackening of powder marks round the tiny hole that showed darkly against his white forehead. There was no need for a doctor's report — one glance at that still figure told its own story.

7

Felix Dexon

For a minute Farringdon stood looking at that motionless form, then he turned to the butler. 'Where are the other servants?' he asked.

'They're all in bed, except Alice, the housemaid. She made the discovery. It was her scream that woke me.'

So it was Alice who had screamed. The reporter had wondered who was responsible for that horrible cry. 'How did she make the discovery?' he asked.

'She had toothache,' explained the butler, 'and came down to get some stuff for it which she had left in the kitchen. She had to pass this room; the door was open and the lights on, and she glanced in. You can see him from the door,' he added, lowering his voice.

'I see.' Farringdon nodded. 'Before the scream didn't you hear anything?'

The butler shook his head. He had heard nothing. Feldon had sent the servants to bed early. He had said that he would put the lights out and lock up. He often did this, so the butler had seen nothing unusual in the order.

'Did he have any visitors this evening?' asked Farringdon.

The man hesitated. 'I couldn't say for certain,' he replied. 'I thought I heard the sound of voices once, just before I went up to my room, but I couldn't be sure.'

'Did you recognise the voices?'

'No, sir.'

'What time was this?'

The butler thought for a moment. 'Must have been between half-past ten and eleven,' he said.

'Didn't you hear any sound — like a shot?'

The man shook his head again. 'No — nothing. I'd just dropped off to sleep when I heard Alice scream. I slipped on a dressing gown and came down and — well, you've seen what I saw.'

Farringdon nodded and looked quickly about the room. 'The footman said you tried to telephone, but couldn't. Is that right?'

'Quite right,' said the butler. 'The instrument is in the hall and I tried to get through to the doctor, but I couldn't get any reply from the exchange.'

'And so far as you know, nobody called to see your master this evening?'

'No, nobody called in the ordinary way.'

Farringdon looked at the man sharply. 'What do you mean by that?' he asked.

'Well, nobody came by the front door,' said the butler. 'If I did hear the sound of voices and there was anybody with him, they must have got in some other way.'

'Is there any other way?'

'Yes, there's a way out through the kitchen. There's another way out along the yew-walk which Mr. Feldon used to use himself.'

'Show me,' said the reporter briefly.

But the doors leading to both these exits were bolted and barred and could not have been closed from the outside.

Farringdon returned to the room of death. 'Was the window open or closed?' he inquired.

'Closed,' said the butler. 'I never touched anything.'

Farringdon went over to it. It was closed but it was not fastened, and could have easily been shut from the outside after the murderer had made his escape.

'You'd better send somebody for the doctor and the police,' he said, coming back to the middle of the room.

The butler went away and Farringdon returned to the window. Very carefully, so as not to obliterate any possible finger marks, he tried the sash. It moved easily and noiselessly, and he was pretty certain that this was the way the killer of Feldon had both come and gone.

He found further confirmation of this theory when he examined the settee which was in the window recess. It was covered in some dark material, and distinctly visible were three dusty footprints. They were big and broad, two lefts and a right. Obviously the settee had been used as a stepping-place from the sill.

There was a stationery rack on the desk, and taking several sheets of the paper it contained, Farringdon carefully covered the prints until such time as the police should make tracings and have the whole surface photographed. Having done this, he began to conduct an examination of the death chamber. Working from the window towards the door, he looked for traces on the thick carpet, but without result. And then he turned his attention to the desk.

He was engaged in looking through the last drawer when there came steps up the passage. The newcomer was the local inspector, a phlegmatic, important man who appeared rather to resent the presence of a newspaper reporter in the zone of his activities. He remarked that it was a very bad business, and Farringdon thought how strange it was that everybody always made that remark on these occasions.

'You haven't disturbed anything, I suppose?' he remarked, when he had taken a brief look at the body.

Farringdon shook his head. 'No, everything is exactly as I found it,' he said. The inspector pursed his thick lips and scratched the back of his neck.

'Seems a pretty mysterious business,'

he said, frowning. 'The second murder we've had in these parts.'

'So I understand,' said Farringdon.

The doctor arrived at that moment, and his examination was brief. 'Quite dead,' he reported. 'The bullet has passed clean through his brain. You ought to find it somewhere in the room. No, he couldn't possibly have done it himself,' — this in answer to the inspector. 'The bullet is in practically a straight line from the centre of his forehead to the back of his head. It would be next to impossible to hold a pistol oneself like that; it would contort the wrist and elbow too much. You try it. Besides, look at his face. He saw death coming on him and it wasn't pleasant.'

The doctor did not stay long, and soon after he had gone the inspector had the body removed and taken upstairs to the dead man's bedroom.

It was Farringdon who found the bullet in the wall just over the mantelpiece, and he brought the twisted piece of metal to the inspector. The official looked at it. 'Fired from an ordinary revolver,' he commented. 'That accounts for the fact that we didn't find a shell. Over the mantelpiece, eh? Must have been fired from the front of the desk.' He slipped the little blob of lead into his pocket and hastily examined the desk. 'There's nothing of any help here,' he announced after a pause, 'but there may be footprints outside the window.' He turned to the butler, who was watching interestedly from the open doorway. 'See that nobody goes near. I want to have a look out there as soon as it is light.'

He went out into the hall and found several people clustered at the foot of the stairs, bombarding the footman with questions. 'What are these people doing here?' he asked sharply.

'They live near, sir,' answered the worried butler, coming to his side. 'They heard the scream and came to see what the matter was. I was just telling Captain Drake — '

'Is this true — that Feldon's been shot?' A tall, white-haired man with close-cropped hair and a fierce military moustache came forward and addressed the inspector.

'Quite true,' said that individual. 'It's a dreadful business.'

'Dreadful indeed,' muttered the other, and Farringdon saw that his face was ghastly.

'Good God, how many more?' A fat, greasy-looking man uttered the remark, and the reporter heard another, who looked like a retired banker, mutter:

'Something was bound to happen, Sopley, though I'm surprised it was Feldon.'

'What do you mean, Earnshaw?' asked the man addressed as Sopley.

Earnshaw looked confused. 'Oh, nothing,' he said evasively. 'Only, I've felt as though there was something in the air lately.'

Farringdon Street's eyes narrowed. He had not been supposed to overhear that muttered conversation, but he had and it made him think. So other people had felt that oppressive atmosphere that seemed to be part and parcel of the Deneswood Estate.

'Ask these gentlemen to wait in the drawing room.' The inspector's voice

79

broke in on his thoughts. 'Since they are here I should like to ask them one or two questions.'

This didn't appear to meet with whole-hearted approval. He noticed several uneasy glances, and was rather surprised.

Mr. Earnshaw put his doubts into words. 'Is that necessary. Inspector?' he asked. 'I mean — we none of us know anything about this affair except that we heard the scream, and it's not a pleasant business to be mixed up with.'

'I'm sorry, sir, but whether it's pleasant or otherwise, I shall have to ask you all to remain,' replied the inspector shortly. He was looking a little harassed.

'Wouldn't the morning do — ' began Mr. Sopley nervously. He broke off as a step sounded on the gravel without and the large form of Mr. Blessington came into the light. He had evidently dressed hurriedly, for he wore a coat over his pyjama jacket.

'What is this I hear?' he asked. 'What is this about poor Feldon? What has happened?'

'A murder has happened, sir,' said the

inspector grimly. 'How did you hear of it?'

'My butler woke me and said something serious had occurred,' replied Mr. Blessington. 'Good gracious! How terrible!' His big face was white and his eyes stared in horror. 'Is it Feldon who has been killed?'

The inspector nodded.

'There seems to be nothing but trouble here!' exclaimed Mr. Blessington. 'The death of that unfortunate tramp was bad enough, but now — it's really horrible — horrible!'

'It's worse for Feldon!' snapped Sopley, and Farringdon grinned to himself, for he rather disliked Mr. Blessington, whose worries were chiefly concerned with the bad publicity that would attach to his beloved property.

'Shut that door!' ordered the inspector. 'We shall have the whole population here if you don't.' He had addressed the butler, and as the man moved forward to obey the order the little group shuffled towards the staircase. The front door was closed, and when this was done the local inspector looked round the group. His eyes came to rest on Farringdon, and he came over to the reporter's side.

'I'd like to have a word with you first,' he said, and he led the way into the study. 'Go and see that none of those people leave.' He jerked his head towards the door, and the constable whom he had brought with him and who had been left in the death room went out into the hall. 'Now, I'd like your name and anything you can tell me about this business,' said the inspector briskly.

Farringdon gave his name and the police official's sandy eyebrows rose.

'I've heard of you, Mr. Street,' he said, and his tone was a little more genial. 'As a matter of fact, I've read quite a lot of your stuff. This is in your line, isn't it?'

'Very much so,' answered the reporter. 'In fact I think I have information regarding this crime that will be of definite value.'

'I'm very glad to hear that — ' began the inspector, and he stopped as there came a dull thudding at the front door. It was the sound of someone beating with an open hand on the woodwork. The inspector pulled open the study door and stepped out into the hall. 'What's that?' he demanded.

'It's somebody at the door, sir,' said the constable.

'See who it is,' ordered his superior, and the man went across and pulled back the catch.

A figure staggered across the threshold: the figure of a tall, emaciated man, whose clothes were in rags. His face was thick with white dust, and his hair unkempt and wild. From one wrist dangled a broken handcuff. He stood blinking in the light, his mouth moving as though he was trying to speak, and Farringdon got the greatest shock of his life as he recognised him.

'Good God! It's Felix Dexon!' he exclaimed, and the words had barely left his lips when the lights went out.

'Who put that light out?' cried the inspector, and Farringdon heard a low 'plop', a thin moan of sound from the darkness, and a fall.

The lights went on again as suddenly as

they had gone out, and the reporter saw the butler was standing by the switch.

'Somebody put the switch up,' he said tremulously, and ended with a gasp as he caught sight of the huddled figure lying on the floor. 'Look!' He pointed at a dark stream that was oozing over the polished parquet.

'Blood!' breathed Farringdon, and striding across stooped over the motionless form. One look he gave at the staring eyes, and then he turned the ragged man gently on his side.

'He's dead,' he said gravely, and they saw where the blood had come from — a small wound over the heart.

8

At the Quarry

'Let all these people into the drawing room,' said the inspector to the white-faced butler. 'Nobody is to leave the house on any pretext whatever. Search them all for firearms, you understand?'

The constable, to whom the latter part of his speech had been addressed, nodded, and a few seconds later the hall was cleared. Only Farringdon remained, and the inspector came over to him as he still bent over the body.

'There's not the slightest doubt that this is Felix Dexon,' muttered the reporter. 'Here, on the side of his neck, is the birthmark that was described in the papers.'

The inspector raised his eyebrows. 'Isn't that the American gentleman who disappeared?' he asked interestedly.

'Yes,' said Farringdon curtly. 'It was

concerning him that I was here. See this broken handcuff, Inspector? It was attached to a staple somewhere and has been dragged out.' He looked at the thin form. 'Whoever has been keeping him prisoner has treated him shamefully.' He pointed to the scars on the skinny arms. 'Look here, and here. They've almost starved him, too.' He examined the feet of the dead man and then he rose. 'He was killed when those lights went out,' he said, biting his lips. 'He couldn't have been shot from outside. He was killed in the hall.'

The inspector's face expressed his surprise. 'What — while we were all here?' he asked incredulously. 'It's impossible!'

'It can't be, because it happened,' answered Farringdon wearily. 'Somebody switched off the lights while our attention was fixed on Dexon and then shot him with a silenced gun. I heard the plop it made.'

'But it's impossible,' declared the inspector again. 'There was only Mr. Sopley, Mr. Earnshaw, Mr. Jones-Perry and Captain Drake here, and it couldn't have been any of those gentlemen.'

'Why not?' said Farringdon.

'Well — ' began the inspector.

'There was also yourself, myself, the butler, the constable and Mr. Blessington,' Farringdon broke in. 'That's eight, and one of those eight was the murderer. I know it wasn't me, and it wasn't you. That leaves six. Now, who out of those six killed Felix Dexon?'

'There's another alternative,' said the inspector, 'and that is that the man who killed Feldon never left the house at all.'

'Yes, that's a possibility,' admitted Farringdon, nodding.

'He may have been hiding somewhere,' the inspector went on, 'and switched out the light so as he could escape by the front door, shooting this fellow because he got in his way.'

'I don't see why he should go to all that trouble when there are several perfectly good windows he could have gone through if he'd wanted to,' objected the reporter. 'I think the idea's a bit far-fetched. The person who killed Dexon killed him because he was afraid of what he might say — the same reason he shot Feldon.'

The inspector remained silent. He was a little annoyed at having his theory exploded in this way, particularly as he considered it was much more far-fetched to suspect any of the extremely respectable residents of Deneswood Valley.

'Is there any limestone round about here?' asked Farringdon, suddenly breaking the silence.

'Limestone?' The inspector scratched his ear. 'There's the old quarry farther down the valley. They used to get limestone from there. It's shut up now — has been for years.'

'That's where he came from,' said the reporter with conviction. 'That's where he's been kept concealed. His clothes and boots are saturated with limestone dust.' He was speaking almost to himself, as though he were verbally tabulating his thoughts. 'They kept him somewhere in the quarry, and tonight he escaped. Now, why did he come here? This would have been the last place he'd have come to if he'd known that Feldon had been connected with his abduction. That's it! He didn't know! He couldn't have known. Whatever Feldon had to do with it, Dexon didn't know, and therefore, when he got free the first place he made for was his friend's house.'

The inspector gaped at him, but before he could say anything the drawing room door opened and the constable appeared. 'I've finished the search, sir,' he reported, 'and there's not a weapon on any of them.'

The inspector gave Farringdon a triumphant look. 'I didn't expect there would be,' he grunted. 'No. I'm pretty sure I was right. The murderer was hiding in the house and shot this fellow as he was escaping. All the same,' he added, 'we'll go and have a look at that quarry as soon as it is light.'

'I'd like to come with you,' said Farririgdon, and the inspector offered no objection.

The local man went into the drawing room and Farringdon followed him. The occupants were grouped silently together, a white-faced and scared quintet, and for nearly an hour the inspector questioned and cross-questioned them, but he received only evasive answers. They were frightened, not because of the crime which had been committed in their midst, but of something else. Try as he would, the reporter couldn't imagine what it was. Of one thing, however, he was certain — each man there, with the possible exception of Mr. Blessington, who kept muttering that the estate was ruined, was concealing something; was afraid of saying too much.

Dawn was breaking when the inspector let them go back to their respective houses and went round to look for traces outside the study window. There were plenty of impressions of the broad-toed shoes both coming and going, but they had all led to the gravel path round the lawn, and here it was impossible to follow them. But they afforded ample proof of the way the killer of Feldon had come and gone.

'You see, he did make use of the window after all,' said Farringdon, and the inspector grunted. 'He may have come back to the house after by the front door — as I firmly believe he did, but after killing Feldon he made his escape by the window.'

An examination of the telephone in the hall showed that the instrument was still out of order. They found nothing the matter with the line until they reached the place where it passed outside the house and here, a few feet away from the front door, they discovered that it had been neatly cut. The inspector had sent for the doctor again, and by the time they had finished their examination he had arrived.

It was getting quite light now, and as soon as the police surgeon had made his report concerning Felix Dexon, Farringdon suggested that they should go to the quarry. The inspector agreed, and before leaving gave his final instructions.

'Nobody is to be admitted,' he said to the constable in charge, 'and no information is to be given to anybody beyond the bare fact that Mr. Feldon was murdered sometime between eleven and midnight last night.'

He joined Farringdon at the head of the drive and they walked towards the gate. 'The quickest way is across the green and over the golf course,' said the inspector, as they came out onto the gravelled road. 'I wonder if we shall find anything there?'

'I'm hoping we shall find the place where Felix Dexon was kept a prisoner for nearly two years,' replied Farringdon, 'and I'm also hoping that there'll be some clue to the people who put him there.'

The sun had not yet succeeded in clearing away the morning mist, and the valley lay bathed in hazy blue vapour, so visibility was difficult. The inspector seemed to know his way, however, for he kept straight on, walking along the fairway of the golf course. They had gone about a mile when he branched off to the right and began picking his way among straggling clumps of gorse. The ground became uneven and lumpy, and then Farringdon got his first view of the quarry. It was carved out of the hillside, a gigantic spoon-like scoop, and the trees had grown thickly round the lip.

'Be careful,' warned the inspector. 'It

dips down this side as well. You'll be on the edge in a minute. It's hidden at present by that bank of gorse.' He went forward more slowly and then stopped and beckoned to the reporter. 'There you are,' he said. 'Unless you know the place pretty well it's dangerous.'

Farringdon came to his side and looked down into the deep basin. From where he stood was a sheer drop, broken here and there with large boulders and clumps of shrubbery. At the bottom, nearly a hundred feet below, he could see some lines of trolley rails, red with rust and broken in many places that disappeared into the dark mouth of a cave-like opening that ran into the hillside. The floor of the place was overgrown with weeds and thistles.

'It looks almost inaccessible,' he commented, and the inspector grinned.

'It would be if it wasn't for that,' he replied, pointing to the left.

Following the direction of his finger, Farringdon saw that a crazy staircase of ladders lashed together had been fixed down the wall of the precipice.

'What's that for?' he asked, for the moment puzzled, and his companion explained.

'The ninth hole of the course is close to here,' he said, 'and, you see, occasionally bad players have driven their balls into the quarry, so this ladder was fixed so that they could get them back again.'

'It doesn't look very safe,' said the reporter.

'I don't think it's used very much,' replied the other. 'Most of the people of the valley would rather lose a ball than go down. The caddies do sometimes — it generally means a good tip.'

'Well, we'll emulate the caddies,' remarked Farringdon, and he moved on towards the crazy structure with the inspector following doubtfully. The ladder swayed unpleasantly as he gingerly descended, but it held, and presently he looked up from firm ground. 'You needn't come down if you don't like the look of it,' he called, and the inspector evidently took this as a reflection on his courage, for without troubling to answer he swung himself over the edge and began the descent.

'Now,' said Farringdon, when the other

was standing panting by his side, 'there seem to be several caves and such-like places in the walls of this quarry, but that big one over there looks the most promising so I think we'll try it first.'

'The place is honeycombed with 'em,' said the inspector. 'Goodness knows how many accidents there'd be if it was public property. Luckily it belongs to the estate, so nobody except the residents ever come here.'

'An ideal spot for keeping a man a prisoner,' murmured the reporter. 'Provided he was well secured he might stop here for years without being dis — '

'Look out!' roared the inspector suddenly, and gripping Farringdon by the arm pulled him away.

There was a slithering, crashing sound and a huge boulder shattered to fragments on the exact spot where they had been standing.

'Thanks,' said Farringdon. 'That's deuced dangerous.'

'It'd be dangerous enough if it had been an accident,' said the inspector grimly, 'but it wasn't!'

Farringdon's eyes narrowed. 'You mean —'
he began.

'There's a man up there who doesn't
appear to like us,' was the reply. 'I saw his
head for an instant a second after he'd
pushed that thing over the edge!'

9

Felix Dexon's Prison

'I suppose you couldn't tell me who it was?' said Farringdon, and the inspector shook his head.

'No,' he replied. 'I only caught a moment's look at him, and against the sky you couldn't see any face at all — nothing but a black blob. I don't know what made me look up but I am very glad I did.'

'So am I,' declared the reporter truthfully. 'Well, it's useless our going up to look for him. By the time we'd got up the ladder he'd be miles away, apart from the fact that if he happens to be armed we should offer him a particularly easy target. Whoever he is, he certainly doesn't let any grass grow under his feet.'

The inspector looked at him curiously. 'Seems to me,' he said after a pause, during which the reporter moved over to a less dangerous spot in case the unknown assailant was still about and decided to try any more stone-dropping, 'that there's a lot more attaching to this business than I know about.'

'There is,' agreed Farringdon. 'As a matter of fact it's a very complicated job.' He thought for a moment. After his first not unnatural gruffness, which was understandable in the circumstances, the local man had proved to be a very decent fellow, and the reporter decided to tell him the whole story. His help would probably be useful in the future.

He listened with interest while Farringdon briefly and concisely told him all he knew, and when he had finished his lips puckered up into a whistle. 'My gosh!' he exclaimed, 'it's a big thing. Have you any idea who the people are at the bottom of it?'

'No.' Farringdon shook his head. 'But I think it's fairly obvious it must be somebody among those who were in the hall at Feldon's house when Dexon was killed.'

'I suppose the Yard'll come into it,'

grunted the inspector. 'It looks to me as though the same person who killed that fellow Lew Miller was responsible for these other murders.'

'I think it's almost certain,' answered Farringdon. 'Though what the motive could have been in Miller's case, I don't know.'

'Perhaps the same as it was in Feldon's case,' suggested the inspector. 'Perhaps he knew too much.'

'That may be it,' agreed the reporter. 'He was looking for a man called Sam Gates, wasn't he?'

'That's right,' said the inspector.

'Then it's ten chances to one,' said Farringdon, 'that this man Gates is the man we want.'

'There isn't anyone of that name in Deneswood Valley,' objected the local man.

'Not of that name,' said Farringdon quickly. 'But it may not be his name — now. You see what I mean? Miller had been in prison. He'd only recently come out when he was killed. Supposing he'd known this man Gates prior to his sentence and tried to find him when he came out. Supposing that he discovered that his friend Gates was living at Deneswood Valley and came to try and get some money out of him — perhaps by blackmail. He asks Blessington, but he doesn't know anybody of the name and Miller goes away. Later he comes back and probably accidentally sees the man he's searching for. He threatens him, and Gates makes an appointment to see him later that night — probably promises him money to keep his mouth shut — and when he comes, kills him. It all fits in.'

'Yes, it all fits in,' agreed the inspector. 'You mean this man Gates is the feller behind this other business.'

'I should think it was more than likely,' said Farringdon.

They had been walking towards the entrance of the tunnel-like aperture while talking, and now the reporter came to a halt and stared into the gloom. The daylight only penetrated for a few yards and then it became as black as a coal cellar. He felt in his pocket for the electric torch he always carried. 'How far does this extend into the hillside?' he asked.

The inspector shook his head. 'I don't know,' he replied. 'I've heard that it goes a goodish way, but I've never been here before myself, so I couldn't say.'

Farringdon pressed the button of his lamp and directed a ray of light into the blackness. 'Well, we'll do a little exploring,' he said. 'Come — ' He paused. Glancing down, he saw that the ground here was inches deep in white limestone dust, and in the dust were the marks of feet. 'These ought to help us,' he said, 'if this dust extends any distance inside. These footprints must have been made by Dexon when he escaped — they are all pointing towards the entrance, there are none going in. This is a bit of luck. It's going to save us a lot of time.'

Stepping carefully so as to avoid obliterating the prints, they entered the tunnel. The footsteps were plainly visible, and Farringdon kept the beam of his light directed downwards. 'There have been other people here as well,' he said. 'Look — you can see other prints going and coming, underneath those of Dexon's, and — yes, by Jove! Look here!' He bent down and pointed to a particularly clear mark. 'The fellow with the broad-toed shoe has been here. These are the same marks as we found on the settee and in Feldon's garden.'

The low-roofed gallery went on straight for about a hundred yards and then it branched into two, one going right and the other left. The footprints turned into the right-hand arm and they followed them. This tunnel started the same size as the main gallery, but as they advanced it got narrower and narrower, and the roof sloped downwards until they were compelled to stoop almost double to avoid bumping their heads.

'We shan't be able to go much further,' gasped the inspector, red-faced from the cramped position he was forced to adopt.

'We shan't need to,' said Farringdon. He played the light of his torch on a narrow opening in the rough wall on their left. 'The footsteps go in here.'

They passed through the slit — it was little more — and found themselves in a small square chamber that had been hewn out of the soft stone. It was roughly square, and in one corner lay a pile of dirty rags.

'Dexon's home!' remarked Farringdon grimly.

There was an upturned box in the centre and on this stood a mug of water and a dirty plate. In one corner lay a pile of empty food tins. The whole place was indescribably dirty and smelt musty and fetid.

'Good God! Surely they didn't keep him here?' cried the inspector. 'Why, it's not fit for an animal!'

The reporter's face was very stern. 'They did,' he said. 'This place was Felix Dexon's home for nearly two years, I'll bet.' He pointed to the wall beside the heap of rags. 'Look! See that ragged hole? That's where the staple was fixed to which he was chained. I suppose they didn't think he'd have the strength to pull it out, or else they didn't take into account the softness of this stone.' He peered about the place, turning over the bedding and looking behind the tins. In a niche, scooped out of the wall, the inspector discovered a writing-pad and a bottle of ink, and with it a pen.

'That's what they forced him to sign his cheques with,' commented the reporter, 'and on that paper he wrote his notes.' He remembered the scars on the emaciated man's arms and shivered inwardly. What hellish torture had been inflicted on Felix Dexon in order to make him sign those cheques and write those letters?

His mind turned to Lesley Thane, and as he thought of her he started. She was Dexon's only living relative. His death meant that she was his heiress. Unless he had made a will leaving his money elsewhere, she would inherit the income that the bank people had been paying out with such monotonous regularity. It was very doubtful if he had made a will. This thought led to another. Dexon's escape and his death would be disastrous to the people who had been drawing his income. Directly the murder became public property, as it must do, the lawyers would take steps to see that the banks stopped further payments, and having gone to such a vast amount of trouble to secure the control of Dexon's money, the people behind this ghastly business were not likely to allow it to slip from their grasp so easily. They would make an attempt to keep that income, and the only way they could do that was through Lesley Thane. The girl had been in danger before, but now that Dexon was dead she was in a hundred times worse danger.

Farringdon continued to help the inspector in his search with his mind full of the possibilities that this fresh aspect had conjured up. The cell-like room was not very large and it didn't take them long to complete a thorough examination. When they had finished the inspector shook his head.

'There's nothing here,' he said. 'We may as well get back.'

'What do you propose doing next?' asked Farringdon as they crawled through the narrow opening.

'I'm going back to Feldon's house,' said the inspector. 'I want to get all the fingerprints of the people who were in the hall when Dexon was shot, and I also want to make another search for the weapon. It wasn't on any of those people so it must be somewhere. The only place I can think of where it was hidden, is in the hall — '

Bang!

The end of his sentence was drowned in a thunderous report.

Bang! Bang!

It was followed by two more in rapid succession. Farringdon saw three vicious stabs of orange flame pierce the darkness ahead, and switching out his torch flung himself flat on his face. 'Get down!' he hissed, and then his eyes and mouth became full of dust as a fourth bullet struck the wall within an inch of his face!

10

The Fingerprint

It was a perilous position, lying there in the narrow confines of the passage with someone in front blazing away at them. It seemed impossible that he could fail to miss them, but curiously enough after the fourth shot there came no more. In the silence that followed the last reverberating echo, Farringdon heard a muttered curse, and his quick brain supplied the reason and also why there were no more shots. The man in the dark had been using an automatic and the mechanism had jammed. There came the sound of rapid stumbling footsteps retreating quickly, and the reporter nudged the inspector. 'Something's gone wrong with his gun,' he whispered. 'Come on, we may get him!'

They hurried forward as fast as they could, but it was difficult to move quickly, crouched up as they had been, and by the time they emerged into the light there was nobody in sight.

'He only came as far as the branched passages,' said the inspector. 'You can see his marks in the dust.' He looked closely at the ground and pointed. 'You see,' he went on, 'it was the same man who killed Feldon.'

'He must have moved pretty quickly,' grunted the reporter. 'He couldn't have reached that ladder and gone up in the time, surely?'

The inspector shook his head. 'No, he's still somewhere about in the quarry,' he answered. 'We'll have a look around. With his gun out of action he's fairly helpless, and we might get him.'

They set about methodically searching every hiding-place, but there was no sign of the killer and eventually they gave it up.

'Wherever he's vanished to, he's done it pretty thoroughly,' remarked Farringdon as they made their way towards the ladder. 'Of course, he may have slipped into any one of those caves — probably knows the place inside out — and we can't search all of them. The place is like a rabbit warren; it would take a dozen men all day to search it thoroughly.'

The inspector agreed, and they ascended the crazy ladder. The man who lay on the narrow ledge halfway up the hillside, concealed by a thick clump of bushes, watched them go with malignant eyes and cursed the useless pistol in his pocket.

The constable who had been left in charge had nothing to report when they got back to Feldon's house. With the help of this man, the inspector went off to make a fresh search for the weapon that had killed Felix Dexon, leaving Farringdon to his own devices.

The reporter decided to have another look round the dead man's study, and entering the long room made a second examination of the desk in the hope that he might find something that had been overlooked on the previous search. He looked carefully for secret drawers, but there were none — at least none that he could discover. He was anxious as soon as possible to get through to the *Morning Herald* to report the two murders, and was rather surprised that the inspector had not prohibited any such action.

Turning away from the desk, he caught sight of the carved cabinet and saw that the door was ajar. Going over, he pulled it open and discovered that it concealed a safe, the door of which was also partly open. From the lock hung a bunch of keys, and pulling the door wide he inspected the safe's interior. If it had ever contained anything, the killer of Feldon had taken the contents with him, for it was now empty.

He was crossing to the door to notify the inspector of his find when that official came quickly into the room. He carried in his hand a revolver, attached to the barrel of which was a long cylinder. 'This is the weapon that killed Dexon,' said the inspector. 'We found it on top of the clock in the hall. The murderer must have put it there immediately after committing the crime.' He spun the cylinders and grunted. 'Two shots have been fired from this,' he announced, 'so I should think it was also the weapon that killed Feldon.'

Farringdon nodded. 'That's why nobody

heard the shot,' he said. 'He used a revolver for that reason. You can't attach a silencer to an automatic pistol.'

The inspector was handling the weapon carefully with a handkerchief, and now he wrapped it up and thrust it in his pocket. 'Maybe there are prints on it that will be useful,' he said. 'So far as I remember, none of the people present were wearing gloves, and the man who fired this has probably left his mark.'

Farringdon told him about the empty safe, and he pursed his lips.

'Looks as though there was something in that safe that might have given him away,' he remarked. 'Well, whatever it was he's got it so it doesn't help us much. I'm going along to get these people's fingerprints and have this gun dusted. If this fellow Sam Gates is at the bottom of the business, as you suggest, and was friendly with Lew Miller, it's ten chances to one that they've got a record at the Yard. If one of the people who were in the hall tonight when Dexon was killed is Sam Gates, his fingerprints should give him away. I'll send them up to the Yard — '

'Why not let me take them?' suggested Farringdon. 'I'm going back to London almost directly. It'll save time.'

The inspector was a little dubious. He was not quite certain how his superiors would view his making use of the assistance of a newspaper reporter, but Farringdon overruled his objections and it was arranged that he should call with the prints at the little hotel where Farringdon had left his car.

He went off on his errand and the reporter made his way back to the inn. The first thing he did was to order breakfast from a surprised and sleepy-eyed servant, and the second was to put through a call to the offices of the *Morning Herald*. Mr. Ebbs had not yet arrived, but Farringdon was lucky to catch the night editor just as he was leaving, and to that interested man he gave a rapid account of the events of the night.

He came into the coffee-room feeling tired and hot-eyed. After a little delay his breakfast was brought to him, and halfway through the meal the inspector put in an appearance. 'I've got the prints,' he said, laying some sheets of paper on the table, and accepting the cup of coffee which Farringdon ordered. 'They're the best I could do. I haven't got a proper finger-print outfit, but I got these with some carbon paper from the typewriter. I think they're clear enough.'

'They look pretty good to me,' said Farringdon, glancing at them. 'These include everybody?'

The local man nodded. 'Except the butler at Feldon's,' he said. 'I'll get his before you go. I had to haul Mr. Blessington out of his bath to get his, and he wasn't too pleased about it either. By the way, I think it's worth making a particular note of Jones-Perry.'

'Why?' asked Farringdon, looking up.

'Because he'd only just got in when I reached his house,' replied the inspector, 'and I noticed that he wore broad-toed shoes and that they were covered with fine white dust.'

Farringdon raised his eyebrows. 'You think he was the man at the quarry?'

'I wouldn't like to go as far as that. But

it struck me as rather queer.'

As soon as he had finished his meal, Farringdon got out his little car and, accompanied by the inspector, drove up to 'Silverleaves'. The butler's fingerprints were added to the collection, to the obvious annoyance and dismay of that dignified personage, and taking leave of the inspector, Farringdon drove to London.

His first call was at Scotland Yard, where he found that Hallick had just arrived, and to that interested and amazed man he sketched his adventures at Deneswood Valley. 'They want you to check up these prints,' he concluded, laying the sheets of paper in front of the Scotland Yard man. 'You may or may not be able to place one of the owners. I'll pop in during the afternoon and find out the result.'

He left Hallick and drove to his flat. He occupied a comfortable suite of rooms in a quiet square at the back of Southampton Row, and here he had a cold bath and changed. By the time he had done this his tiredness had left him. He was anxious to acquaint the girl with the news of her uncle's death, but it was still too early to disturb her, and making himself a cup of coffee he sat down to think things over, and there was quite a lot to think over.

It was a quarter to ten when he arrived at the boarding house kept by the ex-constable, Williams, and the man opened the door to his ring himself. 'Good morning, Mr. Street,' he said with a smile. 'I think we've made the young lady quite comfortable. She's found a friend, too,' he added.

'A friend?' Farringdon frowned questioningly. 'Who's that?'

'He's a young American gentleman she used to know in New York,' explained Williams. 'It seems she cabled to him and told him she was coming over, but he only got the cable last night. He'd been up north on business. They told him at the hotel she'd moved here, and he called yesterday evening to take her out to dinner.'

'H'm, I suppose it's all right,' said Farringdon. 'What's he like?'

'Seems rather a decent chap — you'd never think he was an American,' replied

Williams with unconscious humour. 'Mr. Holt, his name is.'

Farringdon was a little worried. This friend of Lesley Thane's might be all right; on the other hand he might not. He went into the breakfast-room, and presently the girl joined him.

'Have you any news for me, Mr. Street?' she asked when the first greetings were over.

'I have, and I'm afraid it's not good news,' he replied gravely. He told her of Felix Dexon's death and she took it calmly — better than he had expected.

'I'm terribly sorry, Mr. Street,' she said, 'but it's not such a shock as it would have been — I mean, I've been more or less expecting something of the sort.'

He asked her the question which had been in his mind ever since Dexon's death.

'His money will come to me,' she answered quietly. 'He made a will to that effect several years ago, and I don't think he ever altered it.'

'I was afraid of that,' said Farringdon gravely, and she stared at him in surprise.

'Why — ' she began.

'Because,' he interrupted, 'whoever was at the bottom of your uncle's abduction is not going to lose the income he's been drawing if he can possibly help it. You must take every precaution, Miss Thane.'

She understood his meaning and her face paled. 'You're making me feel quite scared,' she said.

'There's no need to be scared,' answered Farringdon, 'provided you take suitable precautions. Don't go out alone at night. You'll be safe enough here. Williams is an ex-policeman and he knows the circumstances. At any rate, until the fact becomes public that you're Dexon's heiress, I don't think these people will make any move.'

'Do you think they're likely to attempt anything then?' she asked.

He nodded. 'I don't think anything is more likely,' he replied, 'and I don't want you to walk out of your house and disappear as your uncle did.'

Before leaving, he called Williams and reiterated the necessity of Lesley Thane being closely guarded.

'You can trust me,' said the ex-policeman

confidently. 'They'll be clever people if they can get at the lady while I'm around.'

The girl had said nothing of her newfound friend, and Farringdon felt a little diffident in questioning her about him. She might quite likely regard it as an impertinence, and to a certain extent she would be right.

He went down to the offices of the *Morning Herald* and found Mr. Ebbs as nearly jovial as it was possible for that taciturn man to be.

'This is good stuff, Street,' he said. 'Fine! Carry on and let me have any fresh developments. This is going to cause a sensation!'

At half-past three Farringdon called at the Yard and found Hallick waiting for him with the information he required.

'We've got no record of any of these,' said the inspector, pushing over five of the slips of paper, 'but we've got a record of this man — and it's a pretty bad one. Here's the card — you can see for yourself.'

Farringdon looked at the official record and read: 'Leonard Schwab, aka Horace

Kennedy, aka Montague Weltman. Five years for fraud, 1902. Served a further sentence, six years, 1909, for forgery. Believed to have been connected with the Inluska Oil Company swindle, 1920, but no proof. Since then has disappeared. Dangerous. Carries firearms.' There followed a long description of the man and full details of his various sentences.

'Whose print does this refer to?' asked Farringdon, laying down the card.

'This fellow,' replied Hallick, and flicked it over.

The print was that of Mr. Sopley!

11

At the Seventh Tee

Mr. Sopley lit a cigar with a hand that shook in spite of his efforts to steady it. Throughout the long hours of the night following the murder of Felix Dexon he had lay staring into the darkness of his bedroom, thoughtful and fearful, and the morning had brought no relief from his uneasiness. Everything was bound to come out now.

He had been in the middle of a pretence at breakfast when the police had called and taken his fingerprints. He had not dared to refuse, and yet he knew that the result would be fatal. In the criminal records at Scotland Yard were duplicates of those prints attached to a dossier that was better left hidden. Mr. Sopley had passed the day, his nerves on edge, starting at every knock, in dread that it heralded the arrival of the men he knew would come sooner or later to question him. But the day dragged on without the fulfilment of his fears, and the dusk of evening began to settle over the valley.

By the last post the letter came, and Mr. Sopley read it several times before consigning it to the blazing fire which, despite the time of year, burned in his sitting-room grate. Perhaps the suggestion it contained was the best way out after all — if there was still time.

He spent the evening going through his desk destroying such papers and documents that might be better unread by prying eyes, and at eleven o'clock, his task completed, rose wearily to his feet. Helping himself to a stiff whisky and soda, he went upstairs to his bedroom and packed a suitcase with the few things he would need. They were not many. His plans necessitated that he should travel light. Once out of the country he could make a fresh start.

Coming back to his sitting room, he unlocked a wall safe and took out a bundle of notes, thrusting them into the hip pocket of his trousers. It was a pity that he could not draw out the balance at his bank, but that was impossible. Anyway, the man he would be meeting later had promised a large sum — a sum that, in addition to the amount he already had, would represent a fairly solid basis upon which to start his new life.

He looked at his watch. Not quite time to start yet.

Pacing up and down the pleasantly furnished room which he was so soon to leave for ever, he smoked the remainder of his cigar. It was half past twelve when he pulled on a light coat, picked up his suitcase, and after a last look round, switched out the lights and quietly let himself out of the house.

The night was fine but dark. Here and there among the trees lights gleamed, showing that some of the residents of the estate were still wakeful. Mr. Sopley made his way down the short drive, keeping on the grass in order to deaden his footsteps, and passed through the low white gate. Crossing the gravel walk, he stepped onto the turf of the central garden and struck off towards the beginning of the golf course. Now that he had left the confines of the house he felt better. The police could come now as soon as they liked; there would be nobody there to answer their questions.

He began to hum a little tune below his breath as he walked along the fairway. A sense of freedom, that was not entirely due to the thought that he would soon be out of the reach of the law, began to take possession of him. Once he was away from the environs of Deneswood Valley, he would be free also from the man who had ruled his life with a hand of fear . . .

He passed the second tee and continued on down the valley. The place of his appointment was the seventh tee, a goodly way yet. His light suitcase offered little inconvenience, and as he swung along he began to make plans for the future.

He would lie low in London until the hue and cry following his disappearance had died down, and then make his way abroad. London was the best place for a wanted man to hide. In that city of teeming millions it was easier to submerge oneself than anywhere else. A slight disguise, and it was doubtful if anyone would be able to recognise him. A great many criminals before Mr. Sopley had suffered from the same delusion. And then one of the warmer climates — South America, perhaps. He had always had a partiality for South America . . .

He reached the seventh tee at last and set down his case. It was very still and dark and there was no sign of the man he had come to meet. He seated himself on the sand-box and took out a cigar. He had barely lighted it and drawn the first mouthful of smoke when the man he was waiting for appeared — a looming figure in the darkness.

'You've decided to take my advice then?' he grunted abruptly, and Mr. Sopley nodded.

'I could do no less whether I wished to or not,' he replied gruffly. 'In this case I did wish to.'

'I think it's the only sensible thing to do,' said the other. 'I thought so immediately I heard that the police had taken everybody's fingerprints, and sent you that note.'

'Out of consideration for my safety,' sneered Mr. Sopley.

'No!' was the retort. 'Out of consideration for my own. I know that if the police questioned you you'd squeal.'

'And you were right,' said Sopley. 'You're playing a dangerous game, Gates, and sooner or later you'll come a crash. You can't always murder your way out of an unpleasant position.'

'Why not?' said Sam Gates coolly. 'They can only hang you once, however many murders you've committed.'

'There is such a thing as conscience — ' began Mr. Sopley, and the other laughed unpleasantly.

'You're not particularly qualified to talk about that,' he said. 'But we're wasting time. I don't want to spend the rest of the night hanging about this golf course.'

'Well, hand over the money you promised and let me go,' answered Sopley. 'I don't want to stop here longer than I can help, I assure you.'

'I've brought it with me. Five thousand pounds,' said his companion.

'That'll do to be going on with,' growled Sopley.

'What do you mean, to be going on

with?' snarled the other. 'It's all you're going to get — '

'Is it?' There was a menace lurking in Mr. Sopley's smooth voice. 'We'll see about that! You've taken a yearly income from me, Gates, because you knew a lot more about me than most people. Now it's my turn. You can't hold the threat of telling the police that Mark Sopley is another name for Montague Weltman because they know already, or will do within the next few hours. But I can tell them who Sam Gates is. A letter written to Scotland Yard would cause quite a sensation in that building. Unless you want to hang, you'll pay me back some of that money I've been forced to hand over to you each year.'

'Blackmail, eh?' whispered Gates softly.

'Poetic justice is a better description,' said Mr. Sopley, feeling very sure of himself. 'I'll take that five thousand to be going on with, and you'll pay a further five thousand each year. I'll let you know where to send it, Gates.'

'Oh, you will?' grunted Sam Gates. 'Do you think I'm going to stand for this, Sopley?'

'You can't help yourself,' said Sopley. 'You've got to shell out or that letter I spoke of will give the heads at Scotland Yard something to think about.'

'You really should have known me better by this time,' murmured the other, and he chuckled . . .

At half past nine on the following morning Inspector Blagdon, who had heard from Hallick, presented himself at Mr. Sopley's house to question the owner regarding what he knew concerning the murders of Feldon and Felix Dexon. But he was disappointed, for Mr. Sopley could not be found. His bed had not been slept in, and a suitcase and several articles of clothing were missing. The inspector went back to the station and a 'hurry' call was sent out with description of the wanted man. At eleven o'clock he was found by a labourer taking a short cut across the golf course on his way to the village to buy a new spade handle. But it is impossible to question a dead man, and Mr. Sopley must have died instantly from the terrible wound in his throat which had almost severed his head from his body.

12

Lesley's Friend

The chief constable of the county which embraced Deneswood Valley within its environs had a conference with Inspector Blagdon following the discovery of Mr. Sopley's body, with the result that Scotland Yard was invited to co-operate with the local police. Inspector Hallick and a sergeant came down and everybody on the estate was subjected to a vigorous examination, but without result.

Mr. Blessington was in despair. Over and over again he reiterated tearfully that the publicity would ruin him, until Hallick got tired of hearing his lamentations. 'It's very unpleasant for everybody, sir,' he said. 'But murder is murder.'

'The newspapers are full of this new crime,' wailed the stout man. 'The *Herald* has even had the audacity to publish a full length portrait of me taken, needless to remark, without my consent — '

'Yes, yes. Most unfortunate,' said the inspector soothingly. 'How came you to accept this man Sopley as one of your tenants? He was a well-known crook and had been in prison — '

'I am horrified whenever I think of it,' declared Mr. Blessington — the interview took place in his study — 'but I can only assure you that his references were unimpeachable. I have always been most careful.' He unlocked a large safe, searched in the interior, and brought out a bulky envelope. From this he took several letters and handed them to Hallick. 'See for yourself,' he said.

The inspector glanced at the documents and was forced to admit that the references were excellent. 'They are all right,' he admitted, 'if they are genuine, which I doubt. There are places in London, Mr. Blessington, where it is possible to obtain the finest references in the world, for any purpose, at the cost of a ten-pound note.'

'I know nothing about such things,' said Mr. Blessington. 'Naturally I accepted these as genuine. When I think of all my trouble and care to keep the estate select . . . '

'The poor old chap can do nothing but bleat about the damage to his pet estate,' said Hallick later to Farringdon Street, in the bar of the village inn. 'I suppose it is a bit hard on him.'

'He'll get over it,' said Farringdon callously, for he rather disliked the stout and selfish Mr. Blessington. 'Have you discovered anything fresh?'

Hallick shook his head. 'No,' he replied. 'There's a killer at large somewhere in this valley, and I'm willing to bet his name's Sam Gates, but that's all I can tell you.'

'I know that myself,' grunted the reporter. 'What's your next move?'

'I'm having every man jack on the estate watched,' answered the inspector, munching a sandwich. 'And I've got one of our fellows at the local telephone exchange listening in to all calls coming from, or received by, the residents, but whether it'll lead to anything or not I don't know.'

That was all he could do, as Farringdon

realised. There was no evidence to warrant more drastic steps, and questioning had resulted in nothing.

'How's that girl of yours?' asked the inspector suddenly. 'You'd better look after her.'

'If you mean Miss Thane,' replied Street a little coldly, 'she is quite all right, and being well looked after.'

'She'll need to be,' said Hallick, unabashed at his tone. 'She's Dexon's heiress, and I'll bet my pension they're after her.'

No one realised this better than Farringdon. Lesley Thane's safety worried him a good deal. 'I don't quite see what they can do,' he said. 'They can't try the same game with her as they did with Dexon. The New York lawyers would refuse to pay.'

Hallick swallowed the contents of a tankard of beer in one prodigious gulp. 'I don't know what they'll do,' he said, wiping his lips. 'But they'll do something. You don't suppose that after all the trouble they've been to over Dexon they're going to see his money slip through their fingers? Not on your life!'

That afternoon, to the dismay and annoyance of the residents of the Deneswood Valley Estate, certain large and bored-looking men took up their positions at varying points and watched stolidly while the protesting inhabitants went about their business or pleasures. Mr. Ambrose Blessington saw these representatives of the law and shook his large head sadly at the invasion of his property.

'I suppose it is necessary,' he remarked to Farringdon Street, whom he met during his evening stroll. 'I should be the last one to — er — attempt to interfere in any way with the machinations of the law, but I sincerely hope that this — er — surveillance will not be long.'

The reporter could offer no suggestion as to when the valley would be relieved of its invaders.

When he got back to London later that evening his first call was at the house at Bloomsbury where Leslie Thane had taken up her abode. Williams informed him that she had gone out to tea with her friend, Mr. Holt, and had not yet returned.

Farringdon was disappointed and a little hurt. He told himself that he was being unreasonable; this fellow was an old friend of the girl's. Probably she had known him for years. Certainly she had known him longer than she had known Farringdon. It was only natural that she should want to go out with him. It must be lonely for her in a country in which she knew no one.

'You're jealous, you great goof!' he said to himself disparagingly.

He was on the point of leaving the house when a taxi drew up and Lesley got out, followed by a youngish-looking man — the reporter put his age at twenty-eight or thirty.

She greeted Farringdon with a smile that set his pulses beating faster, and introduced her companion. 'This is an old friend of mine, Mr. Street,' she said, and Holt gripped the reporter's hand.

'Lesley's told me about you,' he said in a pleasant voice that bore the faintest trace of an American accent, 'and the way you've been looking after her.'

'Won't you come in for a minute?' said

133

the girl as she saw Farringdon's embarrassment, and they followed her into the house. She had read of the fresh tragedy at Deneswood Valley, and was full of questions which the reporter did his best to satisfy.

'It's terrible,' she said. 'All these murders. By the way, I cabled my uncle's lawyers and notified them of his death.'

'The police have also notified them, I believe,' said Farringdon. 'I want to impress upon you, Miss Thane, the necessity of being careful.'

'You've said that before.' She smiled.

'It can't be said too often,' declared the reporter earnestly, 'and the police hold the same view as I do.'

'Do you really think that Miss Thane is in danger?' asked Holt gravely.

'I most certainly do,' answered Farringdon. 'I don't know in what danger. I've tried to imagine what these people who killed Dexon are likely to do and I can't, but I'm certain they will make some attempt to retain their hold over the money.'

'They'll have to be very clever,' said Lesley. 'After what happened to my uncle his lawyers would want a lot of convincing before they paid out any more of his money.'

'Whatever they do will be clever,' declared the reporter. 'Make no mistake about that.'

He and Stanley Holt took their leave shortly after, and the young American walked with Farringdon as far as the Strand. The reporter had taken a liking to Holt at once. There was something very open and honest about him, and he concluded that should the occasion arise he would prove a useful ally.

'If I can do anything to help,' said Holt, as they shook hands at parting, 'don't hesitate to call on me at any time. I'll give you my address.' He took out a wallet and extracted a card which the reporter stowed away in his pocket. Later, when the crisis came, he was to be thankful that he could get in touch with someone on whom he could rely.

After leaving Holt he walked down Fleet Street to the offices of the *Morning Herald*. Mr. Ebbs was in a most cheerful mood. 'This gets better and better,' he said, rubbing his thin hands. 'It was a stroke of luck, that girl coming here the other day. It's supplied us with the finest story ever printed.'

'And it's not over yet,' said Farringdon. 'The best is yet to come, or I'll eat the last edition.'

'You on to something?' The news editor looked at him sharply.

Farringdon shook his head. 'No, but I've got a feeling,' he replied. 'There's a lot more to come yet.'

'More murders?' inquired Mr. Ebbs hopefully.

'I don't know about that,' said the reporter. 'You've had three in the last few days, isn't that enough for you?'

'Can't have too many,' retorted the bloodthirsty Mr. Ebbs. 'Nothing sends up the circulation like a nice juicy murder. The public revels in it. Well, we mustn't grumble, but let me have anything fresh the minute you get hold of it.'

He plunged into the mass of papers in front of him, and Farringdon left him to his labours. Going into the reporters' room, he chatted for a little while with his confrères and then went home.

The last conscious thought in his mind before he fell asleep was of Lesley Thane and the danger which he felt sure might, at any moment, burst out of the shadows that shrouded it and attack her.

13

Before the Storm

The next few days passed without incident. At Deneswood Valley everything was calm and peaceful. The residents carried on with their normal lives, trying to dismiss from their memories the series of tragedies which had given the estate worldwide notoriety. The lull was, had they but known it, only the calm before the storm, the breathless hush before the first peal of thunder. For the unknown forces that had been responsible for the deaths of Feldon, Felix Dexon and Mr. Sopley were gathering to deliver their final blow.

The men whom Hallick had put on to keep a watchful eye on the inhabitants of the estate still remained at their posts, though nothing happened to justify their vigilance. Neither did the listener at the telephone exchange gather any useful information. The calls that came and went were completely innocuous.

The younger members of the community continued to play tennis and golf, and their laughter was the only disturber of the peace of the place. There was one among them, however, whose laughter was a trifle forced and into whose eyes at moments, when she was unobserved, crept a look of worry. Pamela Earnshaw — the girl whom Mr. Blessington had greeted so pleasantly on the day the unfortunate Lew Miller had first appeared — was just a little uneasy. Since the night when the maid's scream had aroused the residents of the estate to the horror that stalked in their midst, her father had changed. His healthy, ruddy colour had given place to a muddy grey, and there were marks beneath his eyes that spoke of lack of sleep. Once she had awakened in the middle of the night to hear his heavy steps pacing the floor of his room, and wondered at the cause of his restlessness. But when she had asked him what was the matter he had impatiently replied that there was nothing, that he was just a little out of sorts.

She had accepted the explanation without further comment but she had not believed it. There was something seriously the matter — something that had begun on the night of the murders . . .

He offered a possible reason for his worry when he called her into his study one afternoon just as she was setting out for tennis. He had not shaved that day; the sunlight falling on his face showed the stubble of his beard. Usually a most particular man about his appearance, the fact gave her fresh cause for alarm.

'Sit down, Pamela,' he said. 'I want to talk to you.'

'I can't stay very long,' she began. 'They're waiting for me — '

'Let them wait!' he snapped impatiently. 'What I have to say is more important than keeping a few young fools waiting.' He was irritable and bad-tempered and she knew from experience that it was useless arguing. Obediently, she sat down and waited for what was to come.

'I want to speak to you seriously about the future,' said Earnshaw, fiddling with a paper-knife on his desk. 'I am not a young man and — well, I should like to see you settled before anything happens to me.'

She stared at him in astonishment. This was the last thing she had expected. 'But — ' she protested, and he silenced her with a gesture.

'Don't interrupt me, please,' he said. 'I have given a lot of thought to the subject and the least you can do is to listen to what I have to say.' He paused and stared out of the window. 'The fact of the matter is,' he went on, his eyes still fixed on the sunlit garden, 'Mr. Blessington has — er — approached me for my consent to — er — pay his address to you . . . '

She gasped. Never in her wildest imaginings would she have associated the stout and prosperous owner of the Deneswood Valley Estate with the softer passions. 'How ridiculous!' she burst out, and her father frowned.

'I don't see that it is ridiculous at all,' he retorted. 'Mr. Blessington is a very estimable gentleman, financially sound, and in my opinion would make an excellent husband — '

'It's absurd!' she broke in. 'I have no

desire to marry, but if I had, Mr. Blessington, however estimable he may be, would be the last person I should choose.'

'All the same, I should like you to consider the matter seriously,' said Earnshaw. 'You have formed no other attachments — at least not to my knowledge.' He looked at her inquiringly, and she shook her head. 'Very well, then, I see no obstacle in the way. Mr. Blessington is in a position to give you a comfortable home and everything you could wish for. In fact, if my wishes count for anything with you, I could wish for nothing better. I won't say anything more just now,' he added hastily, as she opened her lips to reply. 'But please think it over and remember what I have said.' He dismissed her and she went to join her waiting companions with anger in her heart. Her game that afternoon was decidedly erratic.

Coming back to the house for tea, she met the stout figure in the alpaca jacket moving ponderously along the gravel walk. Mr. Blessington raised his immaculate grey hat and smiled his most charming smile. 'A lovely day, Miss Earnshaw,' he said. 'A very lovely day.' From his tone one would have imagined that he was entirely responsible for the glory of the afternoon. She would have passed him with a bare acknowledgment, but he stopped her. 'Has your father spoken to you?' he asked.

'My father frequently speaks to me,' she replied. 'It's a habit in our family.'

If she hoped that this would put him off, she was mistaken. Mr. Blessington failed even to smile at the joke. 'I mean,' he said gravely, 'concerning a matter — er — a matter — er — very dear to me, which I mentioned to him the other day — '

'I'd rather not discuss it, Mr. Blessington,' she interrupted. 'I must go now, or I shall be late for tea.' She turned away but he laid a hand on her arm.

'I don't wish to — er — press my suit at a disadvantageous moment,' he said heavily, 'but I would like you to know that I should esteem it a great honour — '

'I appreciate the honour,' said Pamela untruthfully, 'but really, Mr. Blessington,

I'd rather you didn't mention it again.'

He inclined his head. 'Your wish is my command, Miss Earnshaw,' he said. 'No doubt I have been a little premature in allowing you to become aware of the state of my feelings. I beg you, however, to give the matter your consideration. Your very earnest consideration. In the meanwhile I shall not lose hope.'

He watched her as she hurried towards the drive of Earnshaw's house and then continued slowly and pompously on his way. If the expression of his face was anything to go by, his thoughts were pleasant ones.

★　★　★

Lesley Thane had spent a busy day. That morning a letter had arrived from a firm of solicitors representing her uncle's lawyers in England, acquainting her with the fact that they had been asked to look after her affairs, and requesting that she would call at their offices at eleven o'clock, if convenient to herself. It was convenient, and Lesley duly presented herself at the old house in Bedford Row, of which Messrs. Lavers, Tabb & Lavers leased the first floor. She was shown into a musty office and greeted by the smallest and most dried-up man she had ever seen.

'Sit down, Miss Thane,' he squeaked in a thin, reedy voice, which cracked at the end of every sentence. 'I am glad you have been able to come.'

Lesley sat down, and the dried-up little man pressed a push on his desk.

'Bring the file containing the Dexon documents,' he ordered the clerk who answered the summons, and when that individual had gone on his errand: 'Very sad about your uncle, Miss Thane. Very sad indeed. Dreadful!' Lesley agreed that it was both sad and dreadful. 'I never met him,' went on Mr. Lavers, shaking his head. 'But we handle all Wade & Spelling's English business — they are, as you know, your late uncle's American lawyers — and they communicated with us regarding the contents of his will. I expect you are aware that your uncle left all his property to you?'

Lesley nodded. 'Yes,' she said. 'I was always under that impression.'

'Of course,' said Mr. Lavers, 'we have not got the actual will. That is in the possession of Messrs. Wade & Spellings, and there are certain legal formalities to be complied with before you can actually take over your late uncle's money. In the meanwhile, however, it occurred to me that you might possibly be requiring some money to be going on with, and I shall be very happy if you will draw on us to the extent of your needs.'

'That's very kind of you,' said the girl. 'But I really don't think I require anything at the moment.'

'Don't hesitate to ask me if at any time you do,' said Mr. Lavers. 'We shall be only too happy to act as your bankers until such time as the legal arrangements allow of your taking over your property.'

He proceeded to go into the amount which Felix Dexon had left, and the girl was staggered at its magnitude. She had always known that her uncle was a rich man, but had never been aware of the exact extent of his wealth. The shares and securities had, as the years went by, increased in value, and his income, amounting at the time of his disappearance to nearly four hundred thousand pounds a year, had increased, and was now in the region of half a million. It frightened her a little when she realised that all this money was now hers.

She had an appointment to meet Farringdon Street for lunch and over the meal she told the interested reporter of her interview with the solicitors. When he heard the amount of her income, Farringdon whistled softly. 'It's enough to tempt the Archangel Gabriel!' he said. 'No wonder these people were willing to take risks in the case of Dexon in order to handle a colossal sum like that.'

'Has anything more been discovered?' asked Lesley, and he shook his head.

'No, nothing,' he answered. 'The police are still working on the case, of course. So am I for that matter. But at the present things are more or less at a deadlock.'

He escorted her back to the boarding-house at Bloomsbury and went along to Scotland Yard to see Hallick. The inspector, who was dealing with a mass of reports, shook his head in answer to his question.

'No, nothing fresh,' he said despondently. 'I've been trying to check up on Sam Gates, but we've no information concerning him whatever. If he's a crook, which I've every reason to believe, he's never been through our hands.'

'Blagdon was a little suspicious of Jones-Perry,' said Farringdon. 'Did he tell you?'

'About his shoes being covered with white limestone dust?' asked Hallick. 'Yes, he told me that, and I questioned Perry. But he says that the road along the top of the quarry is thick with it, and he got it walking along there. There is a road along the top of the quarry, and it is covered with white dust, so he may have been truthful.'

'We seem to have come to a dead end,' said the reporter, and Hallick gloomily agreed with him.

'The person behind this business is clever,' he remarked. 'He hasn't left a solitary clue that we can get hold of.'

'What we want to know,' said Farringdon, 'is who Sam Gates is. That's the name by which our unknown murderer was known to Miller, and he came to look for him in Deneswood Valley. One of the residents was called Sam Gates at one time, and that's the man we want.'

'Even that isn't definite,' said Hallick. 'We don't know that it was this fellow Gates who killed Miller; it's only a conjecture. Well, perhaps something'll turn up if we wait patiently.'

His words were prophetic. That night one of the men stationed at Deneswood Valley rang through to the Yard with the information that Mr. Blessington had been savagely attacked while crossing the golf course.

'I'll come down at once,' said the inspector, and three minutes after he had hung up the receiver he was on his way, unaware that what he had just learnt was the prelude to the final act in the drama that was being staged among the rural beauties of Deneswood Valley.

14

Mr. Blessington's Adventure

When Hallick arrived at the house occupied by the owner of the estate, he found it seething with activity. A constable and Inspector Blagdon were downstairs in the study, and from the inspector he received a detailed account of Mr. Blessington's adventure.

He had been down to the village in order to purchase some stamps at the little post office, and on his return had taken the short cut across the golf links. One of the plainclothes men, whose duty it was to keep an eye on every resident of the estate, had followed him to the village, and was trailing him back when he was stopped by a man on a bicycle who had inquired the way to a neighbouring town. By the time the detective had explained, Mr. Blessington was out of sight, but concluding that he had gone back the same way as he had come, the man had continued along the road which led to the entrance of the estate, never imagining that his quarry had turned off by the little lane which led to the links.

It was dusk by this time, and reaching the estate the detective was talking to one of his fellow watchers when they were startled to hear faint cries coming across the central garden from the direction of the golf course. They had hurried to see what the matter was, and had discovered Mr. Blessington, his face and shoulders covered in blood, lying in the fairway in an unconscious condition. He had been struck savagely several times on the head, but there was no sign of his assailant, and although an almost immediate search had been made, the person had not been discovered.

When Mr. Blessington had recovered consciousness, he was able to give but the vaguest account of the mysterious attack. He had been crossing the links when a man had suddenly appeared from the shadow of a little copse of trees. Mr. Blessington, whose eyesight was not of the best, had thought at first that it was one of the detectives on duty in the valley. He had passed him and was continuing on his way, when some instinct made him swing round. The man had changed his course and was almost immediately behind him. A handkerchief covered his face so that it was impossible to recognise him, and before Mr. Blessington could defend himself he had struck at him with a short bludgeon. Mr. Blessington remembered calling for assistance, and then nothing more until he had recovered consciousness in his own house.

'It's lucky your men were about,' said Blagdon, 'otherwise I think we should have had another murder on our hands. He's been pretty badly handled.'

Hallick went upstairs to see the victim of the outrage. A doctor and a nurse were in attendance, and Mr. Blessington, his large head swathed in bandages and another on his plump right hand, lay in his bed against a pile of cushions, his eyes closed and his face almost as white as the pillows on which his head rested.

'A monstrous affair, Inspector!' he said

weakly. 'I might easily have been killed.'

Hallick tried to extract some further information concerning the appearance of his attacker, but this Mr. Blessington was unable to supply.

'Have you any idea why you should have been subjected to this attack?' asked Hallick.

'I haven't the least idea!' declared the stout man. 'I have no enemies, to my knowledge. At least, I hope I haven't. I have always tried to live in peace with my fellow men, and I'm sure there is nobody in the valley who would wish me harm. The thing to me is quite inexplicable.'

It was to Hallick as well, and he was not above saying so to the local inspector when he returned downstairs. 'Why should anyone wish to injure this fellow?' he said, frowning. 'He's a bit of a fool, but quite harmless.'

'The only thing I can think of,' said Blagdon, 'is that he knows something about these murders.'

'If he did, I think he would have told us,' said the inspector.

'I don't mean that he knows it

consciously,' said Blagdon. 'I mean that somehow or other he's stumbled on a clue, and the person responsible for these murders knows he has.'

Hallick pursed his lips. 'Maybe something in the idea,' he said doubtfully. 'Perhaps they're under the impression that that fellow Miller said more than he ought to have done when he met Blessington the day he first came to the estate.'

'That's what I was thinking,' said Blagdon, nodding. 'Anyhow, it's the only reason I can suggest for anyone wishing to harm Mr. Blessington.'

'Unless it was some tramp out for ordinary robbery,' ended Hallick. 'That's the most likely explanation, I should think. Blessington looks a prosperous old boy, and a profitable victim. Probably this fellow bashed him with the idea of running through his pockets and was disturbed by our fellows before he could finish his plan.'

'Maybe,' said Blagdon, but his tone was completely lacking in conviction.

Until quite late that night the search in the valley was continued, but no sign of

Mr. Blessington's assailant was discovered. He had made off on the approach of the plainclothes men and vanished into thin air, taking with him the weapon with which he had struck his victim down.

The search was at its height when Mr. Harold Earnshaw climbed the low fence that separated the grounds of his house from the surrounding country and let himself furtively into the house by way of the French windows of his study. With the curtains drawn and the door locked, he switched on the light, and pouring himself out a stiff whisky and soda, drank it at a gulp.

His hands were trembling and his face was drawn and haggard. The spirit steadied his nerves, and after listening at the door for some time and hearing no sound in the hall outside, he softly unlocked it, peered out, and assuring himself that there was no one in sight, hastily climbed the stairs to his bedroom. Here he locked himself in, pulled the blinds down over the windows, and began to undress. When he had changed completely he stood looking thoughtfully at the rumpled clothes he had taken off. They must be got rid of at once. The question was, how? He came to a decision, and rolling them into a neat bundle, tucked them under his arm and descended once more to his study.

The fire was laid but not lighted, and locking the door he put a match to it. In half an hour or so it was a cheerful blaze, and during that time he occupied himself with a pair of scissors, cutting up the clothes he had brought down into small pieces. When the fire had burnt up to his satisfaction, he began to feed it with these, slowly, one after the other, watching each piece consumed before he added the next.

It took him some time, but eventually it was done. When the last strip of cloth had burned to a charred mass of reddish cinders he heaved a sigh of relief. The jacket and waistcoat of that suit had been spattered with blood, and if it had been found it would have taken a lot of explaining away.

15

What the Gardener Saw

Farringdon Street heard of the outrage and came post-haste to Deneswood, but he was not allowed to see the unfortunate Mr. Blessington. The doctor had left strict orders that his patient was on no account to be disturbed, and all the reporter's attempts to get round the hard-faced nurse were without avail. He had to content himself with an interview with Oliver, the injured man's servant, a portly individual with a great sense of his own importance, in manner and deportment not unlike Mr. Blessington himself.

'It's a very terrible thing to have happened,' he said, shaking his bald head. 'And is likely to have a deleterious effect on the community. This is a very select district. The inhabitants will not relish the sensational publicity accruing from all these unpleasant events.'

He was a man of pompous speech, given to the use of long words and rolling periods. He could suggest no reason for the attack on his master. It was his theory that the assault had been committed by some tramp who was out for personal gain.

Farringdon left him and went back to the car in which he had driven down with Stanley Holt. The young American had been with him when the news had come through, and had offered to accompany him to the valley. The reporter told him the meagre result of his inquiries and Holt pursed his lips.

'I don't see how it can have anything to do with the Dexon business,' he said. 'This man, Blessington, had nothing to do with Dexon.'

'Not so far as we know,' answered Farringdon. 'Maybe the butler's right and it was a tramp.'

They went in search of Hallick and discovered that the inspector had taken up his abode at the inn in the village. He was gloomily drinking beer in the saloon bar when they ran him to earth. 'Hello!'

he said, setting down his tankard. 'You haven't been long in getting here.'

'What do you make of this latest development?' asked the reporter, when he had introduced Holt and fresh drinks had been ordered.

The inspector shook his head. 'I don't make anything of it,' he replied, 'but I'm pretty sure it's mixed up with these murders, and I've decided to stop here until I get to the bottom of it. It's my opinion that Deneswood holds the secret of the Dexon business, and if we ever find it out we shall find it down here.'

Farringdon was inclined to agree with him. He put forward Oliver's suggestion, and Hallick shook his head. 'I considered that aspect,' he said, 'but I've come to the conclusion that there's more in it than that. The object of the attack on Blessington was murder, not robbery.'

'Why should anyone want to murder Blessington?' demanded the reporter.

'I can think of several reasons,' retorted Hallick with a faint smile. 'If I was long in Blessington's company I should want to murder him myself. One thing I'm convinced of, the man who coshed him is a resident on the estate.'

'What makes you think that?' asked Holt.

'He's either a resident or he's known to the residents,' said Hallick. 'He couldn't have got away so easily otherwise. My men have been combing the whole district, and if he was a stranger they would have caught him or found some trace of him, and they've done neither.'

'Have you interviewed the residents?' asked the reporter, and the inspector gave him a pitying look.

'What do you think?' he grunted. 'Do you suppose I've been spending the time in here drinking beer? 'course I've interviewed the residents, and a fat lot of good it did. Somebody's hiding up something and I wish I knew who it was.'

'We knew that Feldon and Sopley knew something,' muttered Farringdon, frowning. 'It seems incredible to believe there's a third.'

'The whole thing's incredible,' growled the inspector, swallowing the remainder of his beer with a gulp. 'But because it's incredible it doesn't mean it's impossible. For all we know, every man jack living on the estate may be mixed up in the affair.'

'That's a bit sweeping, isn't it?' said Stanley Holt.

'Maybe,' agreed Hallick, 'but if you've interviewed 'em you'd feel as I do. They're all scared to death, and they're all afraid of opening their mouths too wide.'

'It's not surprising they're scared,' said Farringdon. 'It's not very nice living in an atmosphere of battle, murder and sudden death.'

'It's not that sort of scare,' said the inspector. 'The impression they give me is that they're all afraid of something coming out. Something they don't want known.'

'But you don't seriously suggest,' said Holt, 'that the residents of Deneswood Valley are all crooks?'

'Something of the sort,' answered Hallick. 'Why not?'

'Sounds a bit far-fetched to me,' said Farringdon, 'though if it was true it would make a first-class story.'

'You're wanted on the phone, Mr. Hallick,' broke in the shrill voice of the rosy-faced barmaid before the inspector could reply.

With a muttered apology, Hallick dived under the flap of the counter and disappeared through an arched opening in the back of the bar. He was gone for barely a minute, and when he came back the gloom had disappeared from his face. 'That was a call from Blagdon,' he explained. 'One of the gardeners on the estate has just called in at the station saying he's got some information concerning something he saw on the night Blessington was attacked. I'm going along there now.'

'Can we come with you?' asked Farringdon quickly.

The inspector hesitated. 'All right,' he said after a moment. 'Come on.'

Holt's car was standing outside the inn, and climbing into this the young American drove them to the small police station. Inspector Blagdon was in the charge room talking to a little wizened man with grey hair and a face that was so

162

wrinkled that it looked like a dried-up apple. The local man greeted Farringdon with a smile. 'Hello, Mr. Street!' he said. 'I didn't know you were down here.'

'I'm everywhere,' said the reporter extravagantly.

'This is Mr. Feener,' went on Blagdon, jerking his head at the nervous figure of the little old man. 'He's one of the gardeners employed by Mr. Blessington to look after the Deneswood Estate, and he says he's got something to tell us.'

'That's right, sir,' said Feener in a thin voice. 'It were the night the guv'nor was bashed on the 'ead — '

'Better come into my office,' interrupted Blagdon. He led the way over to a tiny apartment at the back of the charge room, into which they just managed to squeeze themselves.

'Now,' he said, seating himself behind an untidy desk and pulling a pad of paper towards him. 'Just tell us what it was you saw, Mr. Feener.'

The gardener perched himself uncomfortably on the edge of a chair and rubbed his gnarled hands up and down the knees of his corduroy trousers. 'Well, it was like this,' he began. 'I'd been at work trimmin' the 'edge up at the end of the central garden, and I was on my way 'ome when I remembered that I'd left a pair of shears out. They was a new pair, wot I'd only bought that day, an' I was afeared if it rained durin' the night they'd be spoiled. So I came back to lock 'em up in the shed with the others. I found 'em all right an' I took 'em along to the little tool-shed, which is up at the end of the green, close by where the golf course begins. It was almost dark, and I'd put me shears away and was goin' 'ome when I saw a man come runnin' from the direction of the golf course and cross the path a few 'undred yards in front of me. I couldn't see who it was, but I saw where 'e went to.'

'Where did he go to?' asked Hallick, as the old man paused.

''e went to the fence wot divides Mr. Earnshaw's 'ouse from the rest of the estate,' said Feener. 'An' I saw 'im climb the wall and drop down t'other side.'

'Into Mr. Earnshaw's garden?' asked

164

Blagdon quickly.

The gardener nodded.

'Was it Mr. Earnshaw?' inquired Hallick.

Mr. Feener's head stopped nodding and slowly shook from side to side. 'I couldn't rightly tell yer,' he said. 'I don' know who it was. But 'e disappeared inside Mr. Earnshaw's garden, an' that's all I knows.'

'Why didn't you come forward with this information before?' asked the local inspector.

'I only remembered it this mornin',' explained the gardener. 'I didn't think anythin' of it at the time. I thought per'aps it might be one of the servants who'd gone out on a h'errand and was gettin' back that way to save time. But this mornin', while I was 'aving my breakfast, I spoke about it to the missus, an' she said wot I ought to do was to come an' tell you.'

'She did quite right,' said Blagdon.

'How big was this man you saw?' said Hallick. 'Was he short, tall, thin, stout?'

'Medium,' answered the gardener, 'an'

a bit on the fat side. It weren't unlike Mr. Earnshaw 'isself,' hc added after a pause, 'but I wouldn't like to say it was 'im.'

Hallick shot a quick glance at Farringdon Street. 'Oh, it might have been Mr. Earnshaw, eh?' he said.

'It might 'ave been,' agreed Feener. 'But I ain't sayin' that it was. Don't you go puttin' down that I said it was Mr. Earnshaw, 'cause I told yer I don't know who it was.'

'That's all right, Feener,' said the inspector. 'We shan't put down anything you haven't said. This man you saw came from the direction of the golf course?'

'That's right,' said the gardener.

'And he was running?'

'Well, 'e wasn't exactly runnin',' corrected Feener, 'but 'e was walkin' quick-like.'

They put several more questions, but Mr. Feener could offer no other information. When he had gone Hallick turned to Blagdon. 'I think a visit to this man Earnshaw is indicated,' he said, and the local man nodded.

'Shall we go up now?' he said.

'Might as well,' answered Hallick. 'I

suppose you want to come too?' he added to Farringdon.

'You bet I do,' said the reporter promptly. 'I don't want to miss anything connected with this case.'

'It 'ud be difficult for a blind man to do that,' growled Hallick irritably.

'You mean it's so obvious?' said Stanley Holt in surprise.

'No!' retorted the inspector. 'I mean there's so darned little to miss.'

16

Mr. Earnshaw is Indignant

Pamela Earnshaw learned of Mr. Blessington's mishap with mixed feelings. Her predominant reaction was one of relief. At least, for some time to come, the stout man would have more pressing things to think about than herself, and she was grateful for the postponement. Her father had said nothing further concerning his wishes in this respect, and, indeed, was apparently so preoccupied with some other matter that he barely spoke to her at all. She raised the subject of the attack at breakfast on the morning following its perpetration.

'It's an extraordinary affair altogether,' said Earnshaw absently. 'The place is getting uninhabitable.'

'Why do you think anyone should have assaulted Mr. Blessington?' she asked.

'How do I know?' he answered.

'There's a lot of unpleasant people about these days. You can't open a newspaper without reading an account of someone being attacked. Probably it was an attempted hold-up.'

She thought his tone lacked conviction, but there was something about him that warned her not to pursue the subject. She went about her household duties, however, wondering what possible reason there could be for anyone wishing to injure the placid and peaceful owner of the Deneswood Valley Estate.

It was the morning on which she usually prepared the laundry for collection, and she had checked the linen basket when she decided to take a final look round her father's bedroom. He had a habit of leaving handkerchiefs and oddments strewn about, forgetting to deposit them in the receptacle designed for that purpose. As she had half expected, there was a pair of socks and several handkerchiefs thrown in a corner. She was adding these to the collection of dirty linen when she saw that one of the handkerchiefs was stiff with dried blood.

Apparently her father had met with an accident and had said nothing about it, and a little anxiously she carried her find down to the study.

'Have you hurt yourself — ' she began, holding out the handkerchief, but before she could get any further he snatched it from her with an oath.

'No!' he snapped. 'My — my nose started bleeding rather badly yesterday.' He stuffed the stained handkerchief into his pocket. 'You can't send that to the laundry,' he said. 'It's not in a fit state.'

'They'll be able to wash it,' she said. 'It's one of your best handkerchiefs — '

'I won't have it sent!' he said violently. 'Don't interrupt me now, Pamela. I'm busy.'

She left him, puzzled and a little worried. It seemed foolish to make such a fuss about nothing, and there had been a look in his eyes when he had snatched the handkerchief from her hand that was almost fear.

She sighed. Something had happened to change her father. Something that she didn't understand. Ever since the murder of Clifford Feldon he had been a different man. He had always been a little abrupt and absent-minded, as though some secret worry was bothering him, but recently his irritability had increased to such an extent that it had become almost unbearable. It was silly to be so vehement over the sending of that blood-stained handkerchief to the laundry, as if they weren't used to that sort of thing; and this ridiculous idea of her marrying Mr. Blessington. It was all very difficult and upsetting,

A sudden thought occurred to her, a thought so startling that she felt the blood drain from her face, and was thankful that she was alone. Could that blood-stained handkerchief have anything to do with the attack on the stout man? Was it her father who had been responsible for that?

She put the thought away from her as absurd, almost before it had entered her mind. Of course, it was ridiculous. It was unlikely that he would plead the cause of a man one day and half-kill him the next. No sane person would dream of such a thing. No sane person. The word 'sane' stood out from the others like a single title flashed on a cinema screen. Was her father sane? Was this sudden change in his demeanour the sign of an unbalanced mind?

She gave herself a little shake. This was nonsense, unutterable nonsense. She was letting her imagination run away with her entirely. Her father was as sane as anyone she knew. A little eccentric perhaps, but that was all. No doubt, like many parents, his reason for wishing her to marry Blessington was because of the material benefit such a partnership would give her. In the eyes of the world Mr. Blessington would be a good match. He was rich and in the prime of life. It was only she herself who regarded such a union with repulsion. Like most girls of her age, she had her dreams of the man she would eventually marry. At present he was a shadowy figure without any coherent form, but Mr. Blessington complied with none of the essential qualities which she considered necessary for the man of her choice. Rather would she have considered marriage with one of the scatter-brained youths with whom she played tennis.

She was giving the cook some instructions concerning lunch when a sharp rat-tat-tat came at the door and she went to answer the summons, the maid having gone down to the village in search of some commodities for the kitchen.

Of the three men who stood on the step she recognised two, Inspector Blagdon and the Scotland Yard man, who had been to the house before. The pleasant-faced, rather untidily dressed young man and the other, who sat at the wheel of the car which had been drawn up near the porch, were strangers to her.

'Is Mr. Earnshaw in?' asked Inspector Blagdon, and she nodded. 'We should just like to have a word with him, Miss,' the inspector went on. 'Would you tell him it's Inspector Blagdon and Inspector Hallick.'

'Will you come in?' she said, and her voice was remarkably steady considering the state of her feelings, for the appearance of the two detectives to see Earnshaw had brought all her vague fears to life again.

The three visitors stepped into the hall and she closed the door. She was turning towards the study when the door opened and her father came out.

'What is it?' he demanded, and then, as he recognised the two inspectors: 'Hello, you here again? What do you want?'

'We'd just like to have a word with you, Mr. Earnshaw,' said Hallick smoothly.

The man's eyes darted uneasily from one to the other. 'You'd better come in,' he said, grudgingly, and led the way into the study. 'Now,' he said, seating himself at his desk but making no attempt to offer them chairs, 'what do you want with me?'

Inspector Blagdon cleared his throat. 'Information has reached us, sir,' he began, 'that on the night Mr. Blessington was attacked a man was seen climbing the wall of your garden — '

'A man? Who saw him?' demanded Earnshaw.

'One of the estate gardeners,' said Hallick. 'A man called Feener. He was on his way home when he says he saw this man come from the direction of the golf links and climb the wall dividing your grounds from the rest of the estate. Have you any idea who this man could have been?

'None at all,' said Earnshaw curtly. 'I should think your informant was either drunk or possessed of a vivid imagination.' He had his voice well under control and his eyes met theirs steadily, but Farringdon noticed that the hand that was playing with a pencil on his blotting-pad was unsteady.

'Feener is a very steady old fellow,' said Inspector Blagdon, 'so I don't think the first is a reasonable explanation, sir. You're sure that none of your servants had been down to the village and — '

'My servants do not climb the wall to get into the house,' snapped Earnshaw. 'They come up the drive and go round by the servants' entrance. Besides, none of my male servants was out.'

'I suppose,' said Inspector Hallick thoughtfully, 'it wasn't you, Mr. Earnshaw?'

A frown crossed the heavy face of the man at the desk. 'I am not in the habit of entering my house that way either,' he said shortly. 'Apart from which, I was at

175

home all the evening.' He uttered the lie convincingly and except for the tell-tale hand there was no outward trace of his apprehension, and yet inwardly he was quaking and cursed the sharp eyes of the old man who had seen him return from his expedition.

'I'm pretty sure Feener did see someone, sir,' said Hallick. 'Perhaps Mr. Blessington's assailant hid in your grounds until the search for him had died down.'

'It doesn't sound likely to me,' said Earnshaw, 'but it may be possible.'

'Have you any objection,' continued the inspector, 'to our having a look round?'

For a moment it seemed as though Earnshaw was going to refuse, and the thought certainly did cross his mind. Realising, however, that it would be a foolish move, he grudgingly gave his consent. 'Come out this way,' he said, and rising to his feet he went over and unlatched the French windows.

They followed him out onto the terrace and down the shallow steps that led to the lawn. Crossing this, they came to a paved path that passed under a pergola to a portion of the garden that was a mass of shrubs and trees. Following a winding gravel path that led through the shrubbery, they came eventually to the boundary wall, a low barrier of ivy-covered bricks.

'There's no doubt that somebody did climb here,' said Hallick suddenly, and he pointed to a place where the ivy was torn and broken. Immediately beneath in the soft mould were several clearly marked footprints. The inspector peered at them and followed their direction with his eyes. They led through a tangle of bushes to the narrow path and here they were lost on the hard gravel.

'That bears out Feener's story,' said Blagdon, 'and if these marks weren't made by any member of your household, Mr. Earnshaw, it looks very much to me as if the man who attacked Mr. Blessington escaped through your garden.'

Earnshaw nodded, the frown still on his face. Why in heaven's name hadn't he taken the precaution to obliterate those prints? He thought of the blood-stained suit which he had so carefully destroyed, and felt thankful that that at least was beyond reach of discovery.

'Well, I assure you it was no member of my household,' he declared. 'You can see the servants if you like.'

'I think I'll just have a word with them, if you don't mind,' said Hallick politely, and without a word Earnshaw led the way back to the house.

The telephone began to ring as they crossed the threshold of the French windows and Earnshaw picked up the receiver. 'Hello?' he called, and then, after a pause, 'Hold on a minute, will you?' He turned to Inspector Blagdon. 'They're calling you from the police station,' he said.

The inspector took the receiver from his hand and listened. 'Just a minute,' he said, looking up at Farringdon. 'Your paper wants you.'

The reporter crossed to his side, and as he put the receiver to his ear the metallic voice of Mr. Ebbs came over the wire. 'That you, Street?' said the news editor. 'I've got a man named Williams in the office looking for you. He seems to be worried about that girl.'

Farringdon Street's heart sank. 'Miss Thane? What's happened?' he demanded quickly.

'That's what we want to know,' grunted the news editor. 'Williams says she wasn't in her room this morning. You'd better come back as soon as you can. He seems to think the girl has been kidnapped!'

17

The Night Terror

Lesley Thane remained at home for the rest of the day after Farringdon Street had brought her back from lunch. The excitement of her interview with the lawyer had brought on a slight headache, and this increased as the afternoon wore on and refused to succumb to any of her efforts to banish it. She managed to eat part of the tasty dinner which Mrs. Williams provided, and decided to go to bed early. A long sleep would do her good. Probably this was the result of all the excitement of the last few days. She undressed slowly, swallowed some aspirins and milk which the landlady brought her, and asking that he should not be disturbed in the morning until she rang, turned out the light, and snuggling her head in the pillow, composed herself for sleep.

But sleep was not so easy to woo as she had hoped. A confused medley of thoughts ran riotously through her brain, in spite of all her efforts to make her mind a blank, which she had read was the best prelude to slumber, she found her thoughts constantly recurring to Farringdon Street. He was unlike anyone she had ever met before, and she found herself speculating as to how he spent his spare time, what hobbies interested him, and what sort of home life he had.

At which precise moment conscious thought merged into dreams, she never knew. One minute she was thinking of Farringdon Street and the next, without any feeling of astonishment, she found herself fully clothed and walking along a dark lane talking to Stanley Holt. The young American was impressing upon her the urgent necessity of converting all the money which her uncle had left her into sixpences. In the midst of her argument against this proceeding she discovered that it was not Stanley Holt at all, but her uncle himself who was so vehemently upholding this sixpenny policy. She experienced no surprise that it should be Felix Dexon. It seemed to her the most natural thing in the world that he should be with her.

'If you pile all these sixpences one on the top of the other,' he said, 'you will find that they will reach the moon, and then everything will be all right.'

Even as he spoke he was no longer Felix Dexon but a stranger, and before she could answer he suddenly turned and caught her in his arms. She felt a sudden panic seize her and fought him off, but he only held her the more tightly. Something pricked her arm and dimly she heard a voice say, 'She'll be quiet in a moment.' And then utter blackness flooded her brain.

In the half-darkness of her room a man straightened up from the bed and turned to another who lurked near the open window. 'It's all right,' he whispered, 'she's well away. Show a light, will you?'

The faint illumination of a torch, over the lens of which had been pasted a scrap of tissue-paper, dispersed the gloom. The man by the bed moved over to the door,

182

listened, assured himself that the house was silent, and glanced quickly round the room. His eyes, through the holes in the mask which concealed his face, lighted on the girl's clothes piled on a chair just as she had taken them off.

'Give me a hand, will you?' he said, and working swiftly the two of them proceeded to dress her.

'Have you got the rope?' said the first man when this task had been completed.

The other nodded. From under the long coat he was wearing he produced a coil of thin but strong silk line. With practised fingers the other knotted a loop, made a noose, and slipping it round Lesley's unconscious body, drew it tight under her arms. Going over to the open window, he looked down. A light ladder had been reared against the sill and a third man was dimly visible standing at the foot in the little square of garden at the back of the house.

The man at the window tapped the ladder gently and he looked up. Apparently he understood, for no word was spoken. The man above withdrew his head and came back to the bed. Between them they lifted the limp figure of the girl and carried her over to the window, resting her unconscious form across the sill.

'All right, lower away,' muttered the first man, and with great care they began to pay out the rope, letting the girl slide gently down the ladder to the waiting man below.

When by the slackening of the rope they knew she had reached the ground, they threw the end out of the window and prepared to follow down the ladder.

'No trouble?' muttered the third man as they joined him.

'No trouble at all,' said the man in the mask. 'Easy as kiss your hand. You take the ladder back to the wood-yard and we'll take the girl to the car.'

Lesley Thane felt the sensation of motion. It was a peculiar, soothing sensation, rather pleasant than otherwise, and she gave herself up to it for some time before she realised that it was not conjured up in her dreams but a reality. She was no longer in her bed, and no longer asleep, but semiwakeful and propped up in the corner of some vehicle which was moving swiftly over bumpy roads.

But although she was conscious of this, her mind was still too bemused to worry. She was only aware of a vague curiosity concerning where she was and how she'd got there. It was very strange. She had gone to bed, and presumably gone to sleep. She remembered hazily the stupid and ridiculous dream concerning her uncle and the sixpences. Perhaps this was but an extension of that dream. Perhaps she wasn't really awake after all, but merely dreaming that she was awake. She had had such an experience once before when she had dreamed that she had got up, dressed, and taken a train journey to see a friend, only to wake later to find herself comfortably tucked up in her bed. This must be something of the sort. Really, she was still in her little room at the Williams' house, and would presently wake up to discover that this sense of motion had no reality in fact. All the same, it was a very vivid dream. She could even hear the swish of the tyres and the faint throb of an engine.

She opened her eyes, and as she saw the dim interior of the car and the reflection of the white headlights in front spraying the hedges of the road along which they were travelling, she knew that her first impression had been correct. This was no dream. This was actual fact! By some extraordinary means or other she had been spirited away from her bedroom on this midnight journey.

The combined mists of sleep and the drug which had been administered to her lifted from her brain, and catching a glimpse of the two shadowy figures that sat one on either side of her, she screamed. Instantly a large hand was clapped over her mouth.

'Here, stop that!' said a voice roughly. 'She's come to, Bill.'

'Well, she can't do no harm,' grunted another voice. 'What are you afraid of? We're strong enough to tackle her, aren't we?'

Lesley twisted her head away from the hand over her mouth, a chill fear at her heart. 'What — ' she began huskily, but the man on her right interrupted her.

'Don't you ask no questions, an' keep quiet,' he said harshly, 'an' no harm'll come to you. If you start anything or make a row, you're for it. See?'

'How did I get here?' she muttered.

'I told you not to ask any questions!' he retorted. 'You're here, and that's all that matters. Now shut up an' go to sleep again.'

She decided to keep silent. Her head was aching and she felt a little sick, but her brain was quite clear now and she understood the situation. By some means or other she had been kidnapped while she slept, and these men were the people who had held her uncle prisoner for so long. It was only by a supreme effort that she mastered the fear that welled up within her. Farringdon Street had warned her of her danger, and his warning had proved to be less shadowy than she had imagined. Never for a moment had she dreamed that such an attempt would be made upon her. She had put Street's fears down to undue concern for her safety, to an exaggerated imagination. His repeated warnings that she should not go out alone or after nightfall she had regarded more to please him than because she imagined that there was any real danger, and now the blow had fallen. She was in the hands of the people who had been responsible for her uncle's death.

It was an alarming thought, and it needed all her self-control to face the situation calmly. But she realised that giving way to panic would do no good; might, in fact, precipitate whatever fate lay in store for her.

She glanced sideways through the window but all she could see was flying hedges. They were passing through open country and travelling at a high speed. She would have liked to have questioned the men with her as to their destination, but she concluded that it would be a waste of breath, and sensibly curbed her curiosity.

They passed through a sleeping village and she caught a glimpse of the stolid figure of a policeman standing near a signpost by four cross-roads. There was safety there if only she could attract his attention.

It almost seemed as if the men with her read her thoughts, for once again the big hand was suddenly pressed about her mouth and she was held firmly until the danger was over. When the constable was left some considerable distance behind, the hand was removed from her mouth and her guardians relaxed their vigilance.

She wondered what time it was, and concluded that it couldn't be very late since the sky was still dark, and at that time of the year dawn broke early.

The car turned suddenly into a side road, slowed, and came to a halt. 'Here we are,' grunted the man on her left, and leaning forward he jerked open the door and got out.

'Go on, we're here,' said the other, motioning her to follow, and she descended onto the rutted surface of a lane. The second man followed her, and almost before he had time to close the door the car jerked forward and left them standing by a narrow gate set in the midst of a high and unkempt hedge.

The man who had alighted first took a key from his pocket, inserted it in a rusty padlock, and after some little trouble, succeeded in turning it. The gate was pushed open and the other man took her arm and led her through. For the first time she was able to see that they both wore masks which covered their faces completely from brow to chin.

She was led up a winding drive that twisted between great straggling clumps of bushes, and presently she saw the dim outline of a house — a low, squat building that sprawled ungainly against a screen of trees. There were no lights in any of the windows, and she discovered the reason for this when she saw a tattered estate agent's bill that was pasted on one of the panes. The house was empty.

The man who had opened the gate had preceded them, and by the time they reached the porch he had unlocked and opened the front door. She was pushed into a musty-smelling, dirty hall, and then the door was closed behind her. The man by her side, however, still retained his grip on her arm, and if any thought of escape had occurred to her, an instant's reflection would have shown her that it was useless. In the pitch darkness she heard a match scrape, followed by a feeble glimmer of light as it burst into flame. The man who had struck it held it to the wick of a candle which he had taken from his pocket, and when this spluttered to life she was able to take stock of her surroundings.

As the estate agent's bill had warned her, the house they were in was uninhabited. The square hall was inches thick in dust, and from the damp walls the paper hung in strips, a melancholy and depressing sight.

The man with the candle opened a door on the right and led the way into a big room totally devoid of furniture and in a worse state of repair, if possible, than the hall. Crossing to the mantelpiece, he stuck the candle on it, and going over to the window pulled to and fastened a pair of wooden shutters. 'There,' he said. 'Now you're all snug and comfy.'

She looked at him in dismay. 'You're not — going to leave me here!' she gasped, and the man beside her chuckled.

'You're going to stop here for a time,'

he said, releasing her arm, 'so you'd better make the best of it. There's a packing-case if you want to sit down.' He jerked his head towards a dim corner, and she saw that he alluded to an empty crate which she had not noticed before.

'How long are you going to keep me here?' she demanded, and he chuckled again.

'Not long,' he answered coolly. 'Not as long as you'd like, I expect. When you leave here you'll be taken to a place that's not nearly so pleasant, I can assure you.'

'Don't waste time talking,' said the other man impatiently. 'Come on.'

They both went out, the door swung to, and with a sinking heart Lesley heard the key turned in the lock.

18

Where is Lesley?

Farringdon Street stood in the doorway of Lesley Thane's bedroom and watched Inspector Hallick as he peered about the apartment with a grave and troubled face. Outside on the landing Williams and his wife hovered uncertainly, their faces expressive of their concern.

'It wasn't my fault, Mr. Street,' muttered the perturbed ex-policeman. 'Honest it wasn't. How was I to know anyone'd risk coming after the girl by the window in the middle of the night? I never dreamed of such a thing. I wouldn't 'ave had this happen — '

'Well, it's happened and that's all there is to it!' snapped the reporter curtly. 'I'm not blaming you, Williams, but she's gone and we've got to find her.'

After the receipt of Williams' telephone message he had torn back from Deneswood with Holt and Hallick, and listened in consternation to what the agitated ex-policeman had to tell. It wasn't much, but it was sufficient to thoroughly alarm them all. Mrs. Williams had obeyed the girl's instructions of the previous night and not disturbed her with an early morning cup of tea as had been her usual habit. She explained that Lesley Thane had been suffering from a headache and had gone to bed early, and she was not surprised, therefore, when half-past eleven had come and gone and the girl had made no sign that she wished to be disturbed. Mrs. Williams had concluded that she was sleeping.

'I thought she looked a bit pale and worn, poor dear,' said the buxom woman. 'And I thought it'd do her good if she had a good rest. When twelve o'clock came and she hadn't rung I thought I'd just take a peep, and you could have knocked me down with a feather when I saw that she wasn't in her room. I came straight down to Henry and told him. At first we couldn't believe that anything had happened to her. We just thought she must have got up and gone out, but it was queer; she hadn't had no tea nor any breakfast neither, and 'enry decided that he'd better get in touch with you. We tried your flat but you weren't there, and then he went down to the office. Your boss said you was at Deneswood, and when Henry told him what was the matter he telephoned you at once. We couldn't do nothing more than we did.'

In spite of his fear and alarm, Farringdon was forced to admit this. He exonerated both of them from blame, but throughout their subsequent investigations Williams felt it necessary to reiterate at intervals that he 'couldn't 'ave done no more than he did.'

It only needed a brief examination of the room and of the little square garden at the back to show what had happened. The marks of the ladder were plainly visible, and Hallick guessed that the girl had been taken away by means of the window.

'There's nothing here,' he said despondently, when he had made a close search of the room. 'All we can do is to circulate Miss Thane's description and ask for any information concerning her.'

'Do you expect to get any?' muttered Farringdon.

Hallick shrugged. 'There's nothing else we can do,' he declared.

'Which means, I suppose,' said the reporter, 'that she'll go the same way as Felix Dexon. And the lawyers will presently receive letters written by her, and signed by her, instructing them to forward sums of money to various addresses. And that's all we can do, eh?'

'Can you suggest anything?' said the inspector.

'If I could suggest anything I should have done it,' he said bitterly. 'I foresaw this, Hallick, or something very much like it. We both foresaw it, and yet we let them get her from under our noses.'

'I still can't see why they should have made this move,' said the inspector, frowning. 'It's about the most stupid thing they could do. You don't suppose the lawyers are going to pay up quietly after the Dexon business, do you? Whatever Miss Thane may write, or whatever instructions she may send. They won't do

196

it, Street, and the people who have got her must know they won't. In Felix Dexon's case it was a different matter. They weren't at all sure he wasn't staying away of his own free will, and they had to obey his instructions. There was nothing to prove that he was being kept prisoner or that he was being forced to write those letters. But with Miss Thane it's obvious.'

'The only thing that's obvious to me,' said Farringdon, 'is that these people have got that girl, and that our job is to get her back before any harm comes to her.'

'That's easier said than done,' grunted Hallick practically.

'Do you mean to tell me,' said the reporter, 'that the police are powerless to do anything in a case like this?' That a girl can be spirited away and nothing can be done about it?'

'You can depend upon it that we'll do our best,' said the inspector. 'But we can't work miracles, Street, and you know it. I know how you feel about this,' he added kindly, as he saw the misery in the other's face, 'and you can rest assured that everything that can be done will be done.

I'm going back to the Yard, and in less than two hours every police officer in the country will be looking for Lesley Thane.'

'Pray Heaven they find her!' muttered the reporter. He left Hallick at the door of the house and went down to the offices of the *Morning Herald*. The usually taciturn Mr. Ebbs was openly jubilant.

'What a story!' he said, rubbing his thin hands together. 'What a story! Three murders and a kidnapping! We've had nothing like it for years.'

Farringdon eyed him distastefully. 'Haven't you got any feelings?' he demanded. 'Can't you think of anything except scare headlines and sensational columns?'

The news editor stared at him in unfeigned surprise. 'What's the matter with you?' he grunted. 'This is the first time I've known you come over all sentimental.'

'I'm not sentimental, I'm human!' retorted Farringdon. 'Hasn't it occurred to you that this girl may be in serious trouble, possibly in danger of her life? And all you can do is sit there chortling about it being a good story.'

'What else d'you expect me to do!'

snapped Mr. Ebbs. 'Ain't it a good story? You stop talkin' nonsense, Street, and let me have two columns — '

'Damn your two columns!' exploded Farringdon, and the news editor jumped.

'You've either been drinking or gone crazy!' he barked. 'If it was anyone else but you, Street, I'd fire 'em! What's got hold of you?'

The reporter pulled himself together. After all, from Mr. Ebbs's point of view, it was a good story. The news editor of a London daily cannot afford to be sentimental, at least not in working hours. Neither, for that matter, can a reporter, if he wants to hold his job down.

'I'm sorry,' he said. 'I'm a little rattled. I — I rather liked Miss Thane, and this business has got me on the raw.'

Mr. Ebbs snorted. 'I liked her, too,' he growled. 'But because I liked her doesn't say I'm not going to make a front page story of her disappearance. Get along and turn me in those two columns.'

Farringdon Street made his way to the reporters' room with a heavy heart. He had no relish for his job, but it had to be done. Finding a vacant typewriter, he sat down, cleared his mind of all thought of Lesley Thane as a human being, and set to work to pound out a story. He finished it with a sigh of relief, took it in to the news editor, and when Mr. Ebbs had grunted his approval, left the building to keep an appointment with Stanley Holt.

The young American had had to hurry back to his office, but had arranged to meet Street that afternoon. He found him in the foyer of the hotel they had selected as a meeting-place, full of curiosity to know what discoveries had been made.

'None!' said Farringdon gloomily as he dropped into a chair beside his companion and helped himself to a cigarette. 'Hallick has circulated a description to all stations and that's all. We can't do anything else at present.'

'The people who've got her must be crazy,' muttered Holt. 'What good do they think they're going to do? If they imagine for one moment that the lawyers are going to pay out the same as they did over Felix Dexon, they'll pretty soon find out their mistake.'

He was unconsciously echoing Hallick's opinion, and Farringdon was forced to agree with him. 'It does seem stupid,' he admitted. 'But there you are, they've done it. I expected them to make some move. It was unlikely they'd let Dexon's fortune pass out of their hands without some attempt to retain it, but I never expected anything like this. I thought they'd be a little more subtle.'

'How?' said Holt.

The reported shrugged. 'I don't know,' he confessed. 'I've been trying to think what sort of move they would make, but I couldn't think of any that was feasible. Certainly this is the last thing I should have thought they'd do.'

The first shock of the girl's disappearance was wearing off, and he was beginning to regard it in a saner light. His sense of values was returning, and he saw that the best way to help Lesley was to look at the matter from a practical point of view. It required an effort, but it was the only way. Once he allowed sentiment to get the upper hand he knew that from the point of view of usefulness he would be as much good as nothing at all. The whole of Scotland Yard's intricate organization was bent on the discovery of Lesley Thane's whereabouts, and with this he was forced to be content. If it was humanly possible they would find her, and if they couldn't it was unlikely that he, without their advantages, could do much.

'I'm afraid you're right,' agreed Holt ruefully, when he put this into words. 'We've got absolutely nothing to go on. We don't know who the people were who abducted her, and we don't know where they are likely to have taken her, unless to Deneswood Valley.'

Farringdon shook his head. 'They wouldn't take her there,' he declared. 'They know the place is being watched.'

He had tea with Holt and they talked about the affair from all angles until nearly six o'clock, when the young American had to leave him to keep a business appointment. Farringdon made his way down to Scotland Yard and found Hallick in his cheerless office. The inspector shook his head when he asked if there was any news.

'Nothing definite,' he replied. 'A car was seen just before one o'clock at the corner of the road in which Williams' house is situated. It was a big saloon Buick, and reports have come in of a similar car having been seen going in the direction of Leatherhead. The time fits in. The car was seen in Bloomsbury a little before one, and it passed a constable on the Epsom road just before two. We haven't got the number, unfortunately, but descriptions of the machine have been sent out, and I'm waiting now for any news of it.'

News came through as he finished speaking. A big saloon Buick had been seen at a quarter past two on the outskirts of Shere, heading towards Godalming.

'That's our car,' said Hallick. 'Maybe we'll be able to trace it further.'

'Anything fresh from Deneswood?' asked the reporter.

The inspector shook his head. 'No, nothing,' he answered. 'I've got my men on the watch, and if anything happens I shall hear of it. I'm pretty sure in my own mind that the man the gardener saw was

Earnshaw, but I can't prove it.'

'Why should he want to attack Blessington?' asked Farringdon.

Hallick shrugged. 'Why should anyone want to attack Blessington?' he said a little irritably. 'I don't mind telling you, Street, that this business is getting me down. It's all so disjointed and unnecessary. And this affair of Miss Thane's makes it worse. I've been thinking it over, and it's the maddest thing I've come up against. There's nothing sane about it. You can't imagine any sensible criminal believing for a moment that he is going to get anything out of kidnapping the girl.'

'Perhaps the person behind this business isn't sane,' suggested Farringdon, but Hallick discountenanced the suggestion instantly.

'He's sane enough,' he said. 'He's sane enough to cover his tracks completely, and he was sane enough in the way he dealt with Felix Dexon. No, there's something behind this kidnapping that I don't understand. We believe that it was done so that these people could retain a hold on Dexon's money, but I'm under the impression that it was done for some other purpose.'

'What other purpose?' demanded Farringdon.

Hallick pulled out a cigarette and lighted it. 'I don't know,' he said, blowing out a cloud of smoke. 'It's just a hunch I've got. I believe that we're intended to think that Miss Thane has been taken for the same reason that Dexon was taken. But I'm sure that's not the idea behind it at all. There's something infinitely more subtle than that.'

'So subtle that we can't imagine what it is,' grunted the reporter.

'Exactly,' agreed the inspector.

'H'm! Well, you may be right,' said Farringdon. 'I wish to goodness we knew where she was!'

'You don't wish it any more than I do,' said Hallick fervently. 'But if it's any consolation, I don't believe she's in any danger.'

Farringdon was not so sure of this. He left the Yard a few minutes later and restlessly wandered the streets until sheer fatigue forced him to seek his flat. He had exacted a promise from Hallick to ring him up if anything happened, and at half-past eleven the telephone bell rang. He lifted the receiver hopefully, but it wasn't the inspector's voice that came over the wire. It was Stanley Holt calling to know if he had any news.

Farringdon told him about the car and promised to notify him if anything definite came through. He was dog tired, and after switching the telephone through to his bedroom, wearily sought his bed. In spite of his anxiety regarding Lesley, his head had barely touched the pillow when he fell asleep.

It seemed to him that he had hardly closed his eyes when the shrill summons of the bell near his bed-head startled him to wakefulness. It was Williams's voice that greeted him as he put the receiver to his ear.

'Hello! Is that Mr. Street?' called the ex-policeman. 'Miss Thane's come back, sir!'

19

The Return

Farringdon Street was so surprised that he nearly dropped the telephone. 'Come back?' he echoed. 'When?'

'About two minutes ago, sir,' answered Williams. 'We heard someone knocking at the door and I came down and found Miss Thane in an exhausted condition on the steps. My wife's getting her to bed now.'

'I'll come round,' said the reporter. He slammed the receiver back on its rest, ran his fingers through his disordered hair, and sprang out of bed. His relief that the girl was back was tempered by his amazement. He had been prepared for anything rather than this.

Dressing quickly, he turned once more to the telephone. A call to Scotland Yard put him in touch with the night officer on duty, and from him he learned that

Inspector Hallick had gone home. Briefly he stated his reason for wishing to get in touch with Hallick, and the official at the other end promised to notify the inspector at once.

Swallowing a cup of tea which he hastily brewed, Farringdon left his flat and hurried down the stairs to the street. The dawn was breaking, the sky in the east was pink, and the fresh morning air dispelled the last mists of sleep. He found a taxi on a nearby rank and was driven swiftly to Bloomsbury. Williams opened the door in answer to his ring and ushered him into the sitting room. The man was scantily attired in trousers and a pyjama jacket. His thin hair stuck up ludicrously from his partially bald head.

'My wife's with Miss Thane at the moment, sir,' he said, in answer to the reporter's question. 'I don't think she ought to be disturbed until after she's had a rest. She seems to have had a pretty bad time.'

'You mean she's hurt?' asked Farringdon anxiously.

'Not seriously,' answered Williams. 'It's more exhaustion than anything else. Her right hand has been giving her a little trouble; she seems to have sprained it.'

'Have you sent for a doctor?' asked the reporter.

'I wanted to,' replied the ex-policeman, 'but she wouldn't let me. She said it was nothing. Apparently all she wants to do is to sleep at the moment.'

'That's the best thing she can do,' muttered Farringdon. 'Did she tell you what had happened to her?'

'She hasn't told us anything yet, sir,' said Williams. 'And we haven't bothered her, naturally. I don't think she's in a fit state to be questioned.'

'Well, I'm glad she's back,' said Farringdon thankfully.

'So am I, sir,' said the ex-policeman. 'I've been feeling rather bad about the whole business, being more or less responsible-like for her safety. Would you like some coffee, sir?'

'No, don't trouble,' said Farringdon.

'It's no trouble,' answered the ex-policeman. 'I'm going to make some for myself, as a matter of fact.'

He disappeared into the back regions,

and dropping into a chair the reporter lighted a cigarette. The reappearance of Lesley Thane had lifted a great weight from his mind. Something must have gone wrong somewhere with the schemes of the people who had kidnapped her, and she had contrived to escape. Well, the only thing that really mattered was that she was safe and sound. There was a possibility that her story might help them to trace the persons behind the murder of her uncle and the other crimes.

Williams came back with a steaming jug of coffee, and they were drinking this when Hallick arrived. The news which had been relayed to him had obviously brought him from his bed, for his chin was rough and unshaven and there was evidence that he had dressed hurriedly.

'How soon can I see Miss Thane?' he asked, when he had heard Williams's story. 'I don't want to worry her, but it's essential that I should hear what she has to say as soon as possible.'

'I'll go up and see whether she's asleep,' said the ex-policeman. He went out of the room and they heard his steps ascending the stairs.

'Well, this is an unexpected development,' said Hallick, looking at Farringdon.

The reporter nodded. 'Unexpected, but very pleasant,' he said. 'You don't know how worried I was, Hallick.'

'I do,' said Hallick, yawning. 'I wasn't feeling too easy myself. This'll be a bad blow for the people behind this business. The fact that Miss Thane succeeded in escaping from their clutches is going to upset all their plans. I wonder if she'll be able to tell us anything?'

'Will it be any good if she does?' said Farringdon. 'When they've discovered she's escaped they'll know that any information she has will reach the police, and they'll take precautions. I shouldn't bank too much on that.'

Williams came back before the inspector could reply to inform them that Lesley Thane was awake and would see them. They followed him up the stairs and into the room in which the girl had been put. It was a different room to the one she had occupied before, its windows facing the street.

'I'm not taking any more risks,' said Williams, when Farringdon commented on this. 'As long as she stays here she'll have this room. It's practically impossible for anyone to get at her from outside here.'

The girl was lying back in the bed, with Mrs. Williams fussing round her like an aged hen with a brood of chickens. She was very pale, and there were lines about her face which had not been in evidence before. Her right hand, lying outside the coverlet, was bandaged.

'I hope you're not going to worry me too much,' she said with a tired smile. 'I'm very sleepy, and you don't know how much I want to rest.'

'We won't disturb you longer than is absolutely necessary, Miss Thane,' said Hallick, 'but time is important, and it is essential that you should tell us anything you know at once, so that we can get to work.'

'I realise that,' she said, 'and I can tell you something that I'm sure you will be interested to hear. I can give you a description of the man who is responsible for my uncle's murder.'

'You can?' said Hallick eagerly. 'That's going to be in enormous help. What is he like?'

Her forehead wrinkled in an effort of concentration. 'He's tall and thin,' she said, 'with a yellowish, lined face and grey hair. I should think his age was somewhere in the region of sixty, but he may be older. He speaks with a slightly foreign accent, and his eyes are a very pale shade of blue.'

The inspector noted the description down in a book which he took from his pocket. 'You have no idea of his name?' he asked.

She shook her head. 'No. I can only tell you what he's like,' she answered. 'Would the description apply to anyone in Deneswood Valley?'

'No,' said Hallick. 'There's nobody like that on the estate that we've seen. Now, Miss Thane, tell us how you managed to get back here, and what happened during the time you were missing?'

'Where shall I begin?' she asked, and then, before they had time to answer: 'I'd better start from the moment I recovered consciousness and found myself in the car.'

She gave them a brief account of her unpleasant journey, the arrival at the empty house, and being locked in the big room with only a packing-case for furniture.

'I was terribly frightened,' she went on, 'when the men went away and left me, and very tired. I knew, of course, that the people into whose hands I had fallen were the same who had been responsible for my uncle's murder, and the knowledge didn't add to the pleasantness of the situation. After a little while I began to think about escaping, and made an examination of the room in which I had been shut, but it wasn't long before I saw that my chance of getting away was hopeless. The shutters had been fastened over the window with an iron bar and secured with a new padlock. It was an old house, and both the shutters and the door were solid, apart from which I was pretty certain that the two men who had brought me there had not gone very far away.

'After a little while I began to feel tired, and making myself as comfortable as I could on the packing-case in the corner, I fell asleep. I dozed fitfully on and off through the whole of that interminable night. When I at last awoke I was in darkness. The candle had burnt out, and only a faint glimmer filtered round the shutters over the window. I still felt heavy and unrefreshed, for my sleep had been broken, and it was not very comfortable propped against the wall in the corner. I could hear movements in the house, and presently the door was unlocked and one of the men who had brought me to the place came in with a cup of tea and some bread and butter. I don't think I've ever been more thankful for anything than I was for that cup of tea.' She smiled wryly at the recollection.

'I asked him what they were going to do with me,' she continued, 'but he refused to answer any questions, the same as he had refused on the previous night. All that he would say was that if I lived long enough I'd see, which was not very cheering. I drank the tea and ate the bread and butter, for I was hungry, and he watched me while I did so. When I had finished he took away the plate and the cup and once more locked the door. It was obvious that I could do nothing except make the best of the situation. I don't think I've ever known time pass so slowly. I hadn't got my watch with me, so I had no means of finding out what hour it was. Somewhere round about midday, I suppose, the other man appeared with sandwiches and more tea.

'After this I was left alone for several hours, until, in fact, it was dark, and then both the men came in and informed me that they were taking me away. By that time I was so glad at the prospect of getting out of that dismal room that I made no demur. I did ask where we were going to, but received the same reply as before, that if I waited I'd see. I was taken down the drive to the gate, and here the car was waiting. Into this I was pushed, and the two men took their places on either side of me as they had done on the previous night. This time, however, the blinds were down, so I could see nothing of our direction. We seemed to have been travelling for hours before we eventually stopped and I was ordered to get out.

'I was rather curious to see where I had been brought, but my curiosity was unsatisfied, for all I could see of my surroundings was trees. We seemed to have pulled up at the edge of a small wood. It crossed my mind that we might be somewhere near Deneswood Valley, but I was to discover afterwards that we were close to Godalming. One of the men took my arm and let me through a copse of trees to a field path. We traversed this across a meadow, and passed through a gate into a little lane. It was very narrow, and opposite the field gate was another. I was led over to this, and beyond saw that there was a house of some sort. A flagged path led up to a porch. As we approached, the door was opened and the man I've already described ushered us into a narrow passage.

''Is this the girl?' he grunted, and the man who was holding my arm nodded.

''This is the girl,' he said. 'What do we do with her?'

''Put her in the sitting room,' answered the elderly man, and I was led into a shabby little room which was full of old-fashioned furniture.

''So you're Felix Dexon's niece?' said the thin man, looking at me keenly. 'Well, I hope you're going to be as sensible as your uncle.'

'I don't know why, but he inspired me with more fear than either of the other two. It was his eyes, I think, that were responsible for this. They were so cold and hard.

''What are you going to do with me?' I asked, and he smiled.

''You ought to be able to guess that, young lady,' he said, and then he said to the man who had still held me by the arm: 'Take her upstairs and lock her up.'

'I was dragged out of the room and up a narrow staircase. The other man unlocked a door, and I was thrust into a room which was so dark that I could see nothing. The man who had been holding my arm let go and struck a match, and when he had lighted an oil-lamp I saw that I was in a small bedroom with a sloping ceiling. It was a tiny place, with only a truckle bed, a washstand and a table.

''You'll be all right here,' said the man who had lit the lamp. 'I expect you'll get some food presently.'

'The other man had already gone, and when he followed, closing and locking the door behind him, I was left alone. The room was so cheerless and I was feeling so dispirited that I could have sat on the bed and cried. But it was no use doing that, so I decided to take my mind off by a closer inspection of my prison, which it seemed that this room was likely to be.

'The place to which I had been brought was evidently a cottage, and the room I was in was one of the smaller bedrooms. The door was of thick old oak, an impassable barrier, but there was a tiny window which roused my hopes until I found that it had been screwed up. I peered out and at first I could see nothing; and then, as my eyes grew accustomed to the darkness, I found that I was looking into a small backyard. Below the window was the sloping roof of an outhouse, and it occurred to me that if only I could find some means of opening the window it wouldn't be difficult to reach the ground.

'The thought was so inspiring that I examined the window again to see if there was any possible means of opening it. I quickly discovered that there wasn't. It had been firmly secured with half a dozen screws driven through the sash, and was immovable. But I did find something that offered a gleam of hope. The putty securing the glass was old, and I saw that if I could only scrape it away there was a possibility of being able to remove a whole pane. But to do this I needed some kind of tool, something with a sharp point. I thought I should have to give up the attempt for lack of this, and then I noticed a nail that was sticking out of the wall behind the door. It took me a long time to loosen it, but eventually I succeeded. It was a big nail and just the thing I needed. I listened at the door. Below, I could hear the murmur of voices, and I wondered whether to make my attempt then or wait until later when the house was sleeping. I concluded there would be no harm in experimenting. If anybody came to the, room I should have ample warning of their approach and could reach the bed before they could open the door and pretend to be resting.

'It was easier than I had expected. Beneath the point of the nail the putty crumbled away to dust. An hour's uninterrupted work and the pane would come clean out. I could have danced for joy, for there seemed every likelihood that I should soon be free. I had completed two sides of the window when I heard someone outside the door, and I had barely time to reach the bed when the grey-haired man entered, carrying a tray.

'"I've brought your supper,' he said, setting it down on the table. 'You won't be disturbed again tonight, but in the morning I want to have a long talk with you.'

'My heart was in my mouth. I was terrified lest he should notice what I had been doing, but apparently he had no suspicions. I had been careful to clear up the traces of the putty as I went along so that a casual glance would have told him nothing. But he went out without even looking at the window, and I breathed a sigh of relief.

'The tray of food and tea made me realise how hungry I was, and I drank the tea, and ate the bread and cold meat that he had brought before going on with my task.

'I don't know how long it actually took me to remove the pane of glass, but I had just done so when I heard a clock somewhere in the distance strike one. The voices were still audible from downstairs, and I debated with myself whether it would be better to wait before essaying my escape. After a little thought I decided not to. It seemed to me that this was my best opportunity. Any slight sound I might make would be drowned by the conversation of the men below, whereas if I waited until the house was quiet I might be heard. I managed to squeeze myself through the narrow oblong which the removal of the glass had left and was just able to reach the sloping roof of the outhouse with my feet. For some time I stood clinging to the window-sill, afraid to let go. The roof sloped rather steeply, and I was afraid if I let go of the sill I should slither down and fall. I had to risk it, however, and eventually I did, without mishap.

'From the roof of the outhouse to the ground was no distance, and I never felt more thankful of anything in my life than I did when I found myself standing in the little back garden. A low fence divided it from what appeared to be a wood, and as quickly as I could I made my way towards it. My one idea was to put as much distance between myself and the cottage as possible. Every moment I was afraid I would hear a shout behind me, telling me that my escape had been discovered, but I reached the fence without hearing a sound and climbed over. My foot caught in the top as I was jumping down and I fell into a tangle of weeds and undergrowth, and in putting out my hand to save myself must have sprained my wrist, for an agonizing pain shot up my arm. I had to bite my lips to prevent myself from screaming, which would have been fatal. After a moment or two the pain died down, but the whole of my arm was numbed and useless.

'I found myself in the depths of a wood and I had no idea of which direction to take. As long, however, as I went away from the cottage it didn't seem to matter much, so I set off, walking as quickly as I could.

'Presently the wood came to an end, and I found myself wandering on an apparently endless track of common. I don't know how long I stumbled about trying to find a road or a signpost or anything that would tell me where I was. It must have been a considerable time, for it was getting light before I discovered a highway. I walked along this for miles, or so it seemed to me, and then I came upon a signpost which pointed in the direction from which I had come and said Godalming, three-quarters of a mile. I was considering going back, for I knew that at Godalming I should find a railway station, when I heard the sound of a car and saw the lights coming towards me.

'For a moment I was fearful that it was the men I had escaped from looking for me, and then I saw that it was a lorry. I stopped the driver and asked him where he was going, and when he said London I could have swooned with joy. He agreed to give me a lift, and I climbed up beside him. I must have fallen asleep, because I don't remember any more until he touched my arm and said we were at Covent Garden. It occurred to me then that I ought to give him something, but of course I had no money with me. He was very nice and said it was quite all right, but I think he wondered what on earth I had been up to.

'I walked from Covent Garden to here, and that's all.' She finished her story with a sigh of relief, and for a moment nobody spoke.

'I think you were very lucky to get away, Miss Thane,' said Hallick, breaking the silence. 'Very lucky indeed.'

'I think so, too,' said the girl. 'If you'd seen the eyes of that grey man . . . ' She shivered.

Hallick rose to his feet. 'I'll get through to the Godalming police at once,' he said, 'and see if they can locate that cottage.

Not that I think they'll find anyone. The birds have flown by now.'

She smiled wearily. 'I don't mind what you do as long as you let me sleep,' she said, and they left her.

Hallick hurried off to the Yard, and Farringdon, considerably relieved in his mind, went back to his flat to shave and adjust the discrepancies of his previous hurried toilet. When he had attended to these details he looked up Stanley Holt's number and telephoned the young American. Holt was delighted at the news and full of questions.

As briefly as possible, Farringdon repeated the girl's story, accepted an invitation to dine with him that evening, and rang off.

It was curious, he thought, as he prepared to make his way to the offices of the *Morning Herald*, that he still felt a vague uneasiness. Lesley was back, and the attempts of the unknown people to send her the way of Felix Dexon had failed. There should be no cause for the depression which had settled on him and which he could not shake off.

It is said that civilization has killed the instinct which is every man's natural heritage. This may be true in most cases, but it was certainly not true so far as Farringdon Street was concerned. His instinct was working overtime and refused to give place to reason.

20

The Sniper

The Godalming police succeeded in locating the cottage which the girl had described without much difficulty. It stood in a narrow lane near the fringe of a wood and was the only house within a mile. Hallick went along to the police station and was received by the superintendent of the Godalming police.

'The place belongs to a Mr. Thorpe,' said the local man. 'He's a city gentleman and he only uses it in the summer. At present he's on a holiday at Bournemouth with his wife and daughter.'

'How long has he had the cottage?' asked Hallick.

The superintendent screwed up his face in an effort of thought. 'Let me see now,' he said slowly. 'Must be getting on for six years.'

'Do you know him well?' inquired the inspector.

'No, I can't say as I do,' was the reply. 'But I know of him. There was an epidemic of burglaries around these parts last year, and Mr. Thorpe came to ask if we could put a man on to patrol the lane near his house as it was a lonely place and he was a bit nervous. That's the only time I've seen him.'

'What's he like?' asked the Scotland Yard man, and the description the superintendent gave disappointed him. Mr. Thorpe was stout and red-faced, rather on the short side.

'A typical city gentleman to look at,' concluded the superintendent, though what he meant by this Hallick was a little uncertain. It seemed that the people who had kidnapped Lesley Thane had taken advantage of the owner's absence and used the cottage as a temporary domicile.

Hallick arranged that a telegram should be sent to Mr. Thorpe at Bournemouth recalling him from his holiday, and in company with the superintendent went up to view the cottage. It was a tiny place set in a small garden that at this time of the year was a blaze of colour, although it showed evidence of lack of attention.

There were two rooms on the ground floor and a kitchen, and three upstairs. There was no doubt about its being the right place, for in the smallest of the bedrooms they found the pane of glass which the girl had removed from the window in order to escape. As Hallick had expected, the place was deserted, and although they conducted a thorough search they found nothing that offered a clue to its late occupants. There were some dirty cups and saucers in the kitchen and several soiled plates, and the dregs of tea in the cups testified that they had been used recently.

'It's pretty obvious somebody's been here,' grunted the superintendent. 'I wonder who it could have been?'

Hallick would have given quite a lot to have been able to answer this question. The thin, grey-haired man whom the girl had described was a mystery. Apparently he was the prime mover behind the whole business, and yet his description fitted no one the inspector had yet come in contact with. As a matter of fact, he rather upset Hallick's preconceived theories, for he had been convinced that one of the residents of Deneswood Valley was the person they were after. Lew Miller had come to the valley to find Sam Gates and had evidently been under the impression that he would find him there. Was this elderly man with the pale blue eyes Sam Gates? Or wasn't Sam Gates the presiding genius after all?

Hallick was completely at sea, and the knowledge did not add to his cheerfulness.

After completing a search of the cottage without any reward for his diligence, he turned his attention to the garden. It was just possible that there might be something here, but he was none too sanguine. It was a beautiful day with the sun pouring down from a cloudless sky, and by the time he had finished he was both hot and irritable. 'Absolutely nothing!' he growled.

The local superintendent was sympathetic. 'Pity that girl didn't come to the station after she got away,' he said. 'If she'd come straight to us we might have been in time to catch these fellows.'

'Well, she didn't, so it's no use talking

about that now,' grunted the inspector. 'There's nothing more we can do here. I'll see Mr. Thorpe when he comes back, though I doubt if that's going to help us much. In the meantime you might put a man on to keep an eye on the place — ' He broke off as there came a sharp crack from the depths of the little wood and something whined viciously past his ear. A second and a third bullet followed in rapid succession.

The local superintendent gave a gasp of surprise and alarm and dragged his companion into the cover of the outhouse. 'My God!' he whispered. 'Somebody's shootin' at us from the wood!'

Even as he spoke, a fourth bullet scarred a white mark on the wall beside them. Hallick's face was grim. Evidently they had been expected, and somebody had been sent to await their arrival in the little wood that adjoined the cottage.

The shooting had ceased, but the superintendent was none too certain that it was safe to come out from their temporary shelter. The sniper might still be lurking there, waiting for them to show themselves. He allowed five minutes to pass and then cautiously took a step forward. How right he had been in his conjecture was proved, for he had barely advanced a foot beyond the wall of the outhouse when there came a vicious 'crack-crack' and two more bullets sang past his head. He retreated quickly.

'It's the first time I've experienced anything like this,' muttered the superintendent, wiping his moist face.

'It's not the first time I have,' growled Hallick, 'but use has never accustomed me to it. Come on. We'll go through the cottage and leave by the front. I don't suppose they've got anybody there. If they had they'd have taken a pop at us as we entered.'

He pushed open the back door and they made their way through the little kitchen and along the passage to the front. Hallick was taking no risks and he opened the door cautiously, ready to spring back at the first sound of a shot. But there was nothing of the sort.

They came down the paved path and halted in the little lane. 'You wait here,' said Hallick. 'I'm going to see if I can locate that shooter.'

The superintendent uttered a protest. 'It's a bit dangerous, isn't it?' he said. 'He's armed and you're not — '

He addressed the rest of his remark to empty air, for the inspector was already making his way towards the wood. He entered the shadow of the trees cautiously, his senses alert for the slightest sound that would warn him of the whereabouts of the man he was seeking. But beyond the rustle of the leaves as they stirred in the light breeze, he heard nothing. For some time he explored that portion of the wood overlooking the garden of the cottage, but there was nobody there. The sniper had gone.

He rejoined his uneasy companion at the little gate, and the superintendent made no effort to hide his relief at his return. 'Did you see anything of him?' he asked.

Hallick shook his head. 'No, not a sign,' he answered. 'Come on, we'll go back to the station.'

At the station they found a telegram awaiting them in reply to the one that had been sent to Mr. Thorpe. It stated briefly that that gentleman was returning immediately and would reach Godalming at nine o'clock.

'And that's all we can do for the moment,' said Hallick. 'I'm going back to town, but I'll be along this evening to interview your Mr. Thorpe.'

He had only been in his office at Scotland Yard about five minutes when Farringdon Street arrived. The reporter listened with interest to his adventures at the cottage. 'More sensational news to delight the heart of old Ebbs,' he commented. 'That fellow's having the time of his life. He says this case is the answer to every news editor's prayer since newspapers were invented.'

'And I suppose,' growled Hallick sarcastically, 'that if I'd been filled with bullet-holes he'd have given a party!'

Farringdon chuckled. 'You're nearly right,' he admitted. 'I've never seen him so happy before in my life.'

The reports from the men who had been stationed at Deneswood Valley were waiting on Hallick's desk, and he glanced through them. Everything in that salubrious district was apparently quiet, for the reports were brief and entirely negative. The inspector pitched them into a desk-basket and lighted a cigarette.

'I've been in the police force for thirty-five years,' he remarked wearily, 'but I've never struck anything like this business before. Who's this thin fellow that Miss Thane was talking about?'

'Apparently he's the King Pippin of the bunch,' said Farringdon.

'But who is he?' growled Hallick.

The reporter shrugged. 'Ask me,' he replied.

'Well, I've circulated his description throughout the country,' said the inspector, 'and unless he's cleverer than most crooks it shouldn't be long before we pull him in.'

Farringdon left him soon after and went down to the *Herald* offices to write up an account of the latest development for the morning edition. At half past eight he turned into the foyer of the Ritz-Carlton to keep his dinner engagement with Stanley Holt. He was a little late but the young

American had not arrived. To Farringdon's surprise and irritation, he did not put in an appearance at all. The reporter waited from half past eight till half past nine, and then he telephoned through to Holt's private address. The servant who answered the call had seen nothing of his master since the morning.

Farringdon ate a solitary dinner in the grill-room, annoyed at the non-appearance of the man he had expected to meet, and never for an instant did it occur to him that Holt had failed to keep the appointment from any other reason than that he had forgotten all about it. Had he been aware of the real reason for the young American's non-appearance he would not have lingered so long over the meal, but would have dashed post-haste to Deneswood Valley, where at that moment his friend was facing the greatest danger he had ever experienced in his uneventful life.

21

Holt Meets Trouble

Stanley Holt was Managing Director of G.I.C. Publicity Services, whose offices occupied a portion of a large block of buildings in the Strand. What the initials G.I.C. stood for, nobody knew. It had been called that when Holt had taken it over — a moribund company whose old-fashioned policy had brought it to the edge of extinction. Under the young American's dynamic management, however, it had recovered, until now it was one of the few publicity services that really mattered. G.I.C., under Holt's auspices, had been responsible for boosting 'Velvet Face Cream, the sex-appeal skin-food'; 'Rainbow Hair Tonic, the dye with a difference'; 'Vital, the rejuvenator that defeats time', and a host of other products.

On the morning of Lesley Thane's

return he went down to his office after his conversation with Farringdon Street, his mind full of the curious business in which he had become entangled. He had been worried about his little American friend, almost as worried as Farringdon Street, but now that the anxiety concerning her had evaporated, he found his thoughts centring on the girl he had seen during his brief visit to Deneswood valley.

He had only caught one glimpse of Pamela Earnshaw, but that one glimpse had been sufficient to register her permanently in his mind. He thought she was the loveliest girl he had ever seen, and the vision of her had been all too brief. During the morning he had artists' drawings to see, copy to pass, and an interview with an important new client who was contemplating a series of advertisements to boost a special brand of cigarettes. But although he attended to his work conscientiously, at the back of his mind he was casting round for an excuse to see this girl again who had attracted him so intensely.

At three o'clock in the afternoon he made his decision. Ringing for his secretary, he rapidly dictated the letters that had to go out by that evening's post and waited impatiently while they were typed and brought to him for signature. Then, making the excuse that he had an important conference to attend and would not be back that day, he left the office and went in search of his car.

It was one of those afternoons in early summer when the call of the open air was insistent. He drove through the crowded streets of London with his whole being aching for the sight of green fields and waving trees. The picture of Deneswood Valley in all its sylvan beauty rose before his eyes, and he hummed a little tune below his breath from the sheer joy of being alive. The hot, paved streets and traffic, the shops and blocks of flats, gave place to tree-lined roads and cool villas set amid gardens of blazing colour. The perfume of roses greeted his nostrils and swept away the artificial scents of the West End, the fumes of petrol and the tarry smell of baking streets.

He came to the outskirts of Deneswood shortly after half past four, and now that he had reached his objective he was a little disconcerted. The private entrance to the estate loomed up before him and he slowed to a crawl, searching his mind to think of some excuse by which he could make the acquaintance of the girl he had seen on his previous visit. He knew her name was Pamela Earnshaw — so much he had learned from Farringdon Street — but such a meagre knowledge was insufficient to justify him in making a closer acquaintance.

He brought the car to a stop and lit a cigarette. Now that he was here, he realised how wild and ridiculous had been the sudden urge which had prompted the journey. He had as much hope of seeing the girl as he had of meeting the Archangel Gabriel. The best thing he could do would be to find a comfortable-looking inn, have some tea, and return to London in time to keep his appointment with Farringdon. Although reason told him this was the most sensible course to pursue, he still lingered.

A stocky, broad-shouldered man who was strolling slowly along the gravel path leading to the estate eyed him suspiciously, and Holt concluded, rightly, that this was one of the plainclothes detectives whom Hallick had left to watch over the residents of the community.

He had smoked his cigarette to the last inch and was in the point of throwing it away preparatory to driving on when he saw the girl who occupied his thoughts coming towards him. She was carrying two books under her arm, and as she turned out of the private road into the main thoroughfare she glanced at him, and recognition came to her eyes. Acting on an impulse, Holt raised his hat and smiled.

'Good afternoon, Miss Earnshaw,' he said. 'It's a lovely day, isn't it?'

Pamela hesitated. She had recognised both the car and its occupant instantly. 'It's rather hot,' she said, eyeing the bare-headed young man who stood before her approvingly.

'I suppose you'd call it hot in England,' he said, smiling, 'but we shouldn't think this was hot in the States.'

'You're American?' she said, though she

242

had guessed he was from his slight accent, and he nodded.

'It's a long time since I saw New York,' he replied, 'but I'm American all right, born and bred. Can I drive you anywhere?' He was determined that this heaven-sent meeting should be prolonged if possible.

She glanced from the car to the books in her hand. 'I was going down to the library at Deneswood,' she said. 'Yes, I'd be glad if you'd drop me there.'

He had no idea where the library in Deneswood was, but he would have been quite prepared to drive to John o' Groats if she had suggested it. He opened the door and she stepped in, settling herself in the seat beside the wheel.

'You'll have to show me the way,' he said, as he pressed the starter and the engine hummed to life.

She directed him, and swinging the car round he drove back the way he had come, turning off at the crossroads and taking the secondary road that led to the village of Deneswood, as it was still referred to by the residents of the village, although it had long since outgrown such a description. The High Street, which had once consisted of small, poky shops and labourers' cottages, had become a broad thoroughfare, lined with more pretentious establishments.

Outside a branch of W. H. Smith & Sons he brought the car to a stop

'It's awfully kind of you,' said Pamela, as she got out. 'Thank you so much — ' She hesitated, and he realised that she was unaware of his name.

'I'll wait for you and drive you back,' he said.

'Oh, I couldn't bother you to do that,' said the girl. 'Besides, I may be some time.'

'I don't mind how long you are. I'll wait,' said Holt determinedly, and she smiled.

'All right then,' she said. 'It's terribly nice of you.' She disappeared inside the building, and Holt waited, marvelling at the extraordinary luck which had been vouchsafed him. It seemed almost as if his impulse in coming to Deneswood that afternoon had been prompted by a subconscious knowledge that he would realise his hopes.

She was gone barely ten minutes, and when she came back he put into words an idea which had occurred to him during her absence. 'Look here,' he said, 'are you in a hurry?' And before she could reply: 'Suppose we have some tea somewhere? There must be some sort of a hotel near here.'

'There is,' she said. 'But really I don't think I ought to. I don't know you very well, do I?' Her eyes were laughing and he took courage.

'The labourer is worthy of his hire, Miss Earnshaw,' he said. 'At least if you have tea with me you will know me better.'

She made up her mind quickly. She liked this good-looking young American whose manners were so unconventional. Liked him all the more because he was unconventional. It was a relief from the rather staid and stodgy people with whom she daily came in contact.

'All right,' she said. 'I'll have tea with you on one condition.'

'I'll agree to it,' he said promptly. 'What is it?'

'That you tell me your name. I really must study the proprieties to that extent.'

He told her, and she suggested a hotel two miles further along the road where they served tea in the garden.

It was curious, she thought as they drove along, that she felt more at home with this man than anyone she'd ever met. Although he was in reality a stranger, it seemed to her that she had known him quite a long time.

They chatted about a variety of subjects over the tea which was brought to them in the rose-decked garden of the Anchor, and she found her companion an interesting conversationalist. He had seen many places and many countries, and his quick observation had noted and memorised the most interesting points of each. The time passed quickly, and it was with a start of surprise that she looked at her watch and discovered that it was nearly half past six.

'I'd no idea it was so late,' she said. 'I must be getting back.'

He beckoned for the bill, paid it, and they strolled towards the car. Tactfully, he had omitted to mention anything about the tragedies that had occurred in Deneswood Valley, and Pamela had not brought the subject up. She stopped him at the entrance to the private road and got out.

'Don't trouble to come any further,' she said, and he guessed that she had no wish for the residents of the estate to know where she had been. 'It was awfully nice of you, and I've enjoyed it so much.'

'Then I hope you'll repeat the dose,' he said. 'Let me come and call for you tomorrow — '

'I'll come out with you again, but not quite so quickly as that,' she said.

'When?' he asked boldly.

'I don't know,' said Pamela. 'Can't I — can't I ring you up somewhere?'

'Whenever you like,' he said, and pulling a wallet from his pocket he gave her a card. 'Either of those numbers will find me.'

She stowed it away in her bag. 'I really must go now,' she said. 'Goodbye, and thanks again.'

He watched her turn into the private road, feeling absurdly elated. It was too early to return to London yet, and he had no wish to do so. He felt more in tune with the peace of the country than the roar and bustle of the city. He decided to explore the neighbourhood a little, and starting the car sent it running smoothly along the road that led past the entrance to the Deneswood Estate.

After a little while he came to the foot of a slope which rose steeply, lined on one side by the fringe of a thick wood and on the other by gorse-covered common land. He was rather sorry that he had made an appointment to meet Farringdon that evening for dinner. He would have liked to have gone on and on, enjoying to the full the beauty of the summer evening.

The road curved to the left and he caught a glimpse of the quarry which Farringdon had mentioned as being the place where Felix Dexon had been kept prisoner. A sudden desire to explore it took possession of him, and he glanced at his watch. It was seven o'clock. If he started to return in half an hour or so, he could make it.

He turned the car and sent it bumping

over the strip of common land, bringing it to a halt at the side of a clump of gorse. A few yards away he could see the uneven lip of the quarry and made his way towards it. A few seconds later he was gazing down into the deep pit with its rock-strewn bottom and rusty rails. Away on the other side was the crazy ladder which Inspector Blagdon and the reporter had descended on the morning they had made the discovery of Felix Dexon's prison. That side of the pit fell sheer, but the place where he was standing was less difficult to negotiate. He decided it would not be very difficult to reach the bottom; a few yards from where he stood the wall sloped at an appreciable angle, and there were jutting pieces of rock that would supply foot- and hand-holds.

He began to make his way downwards. It was not easy. Twice his feet slipped and he slithered several yards before he could check his fall. Eventually he reached the bottom, dusty but uninjured. From where he now stood he could see the cave-like opening which Farringdon had described, and the walls of the place were dotted with several smaller caves. He set off towards the bigger aperture, and was halfway across the boulder-strewn bed of the quarry when he tripped on a loose stone. He tried to save himself but fell headlong. His forehead came in violent contact with the sharp edge of a jagged rock. A brilliant flash of orange white light burst before his eyes, and then everything went black.

22

The Prisoner

Stanley Holt came to himself with a groan. It was quite dark and the stars were out overhead. His head ached unpleasantly, and it was some seconds before he was able to sit up. He looked at his watch. The illuminated dial showed it was a few minutes after seven, and holding it to his ear he discovered that it had stopped. It must have stopped at the moment he had fallen. Probably the shock was responsible for that. He scrambled to his feet, feeling sick and dizzy, and remembered his appointment with Farringdon. It must be long past half past eight and he wondered what the reporter would be thinking.

He was in the act of making his way unsteadily towards the place where he had descended into the quarry when he saw a light flash momentarily in the direction of the crazy ladder. He stopped, thinking at first it was a trick of his imagination, and then he saw it again. It came from the floor of the quarry, and it was moving over towards the cave-like opening in the wall. There was no mistaking what it was. It came from a torch, and the rays reflecting back from the stone dimly silhouetted the figure of a man. He was making his way across the uneven bottom of the pit, and Holt caught his breath and crouched to cover behind a stumpy bush. It might be one of the detectives who were on duty in the valley. On the other hand, he might be on the verge of a discovery. It would do no harm to watch and see what the man did.

The light winked again twice, drawing ever nearer to the arched opening, and presently as the young American watched he saw the man and the torch disappear within.

Regardless of his throbbing head, Holt set off cautiously in the same direction. It was difficult going, for the floor of the quarry was uneven and filled with huge, irregular masses of rock and stone, and covered with weeds and stunted shrubs, and although the side of the cave looked near it was a great distance in reality. He reached it at length, however, and paused at the mouth of the entrance. There was no sign of the man or the torch, and he approached carefully, entered the dark aperture, and stopped, listening.

Dead silence greeted his straining ears, and then faintly he thought he heard the sound of a voice — a man's voice.

Noiselessly he advanced, feeling his way along the wall. A few yards further the roof dipped, and he had to stoop to avoid bumping his head. The intermittent rumble of the voice still came to his ears, but there was no sign of a light or any other evidence of a human presence.

Presently he came to a place where the gallery divided into two, and he stopped, wondering which way to take. The voice had ceased, too. Everything was silent. Then as he listened it began again. It came from the left-hand tunnel, and into this he turned. After several yards it widened and then took a sharp bend to the left.

As he rounded the bend he saw before him a glimmer of light, and then a little further on he stopped dead and looked in amazement at the sight that met his gaze.

The passage widened into a big, cave-like chamber hewn out of the rocky hillside. It was so vast that the walls and roof were lost in gloomy darkness. In the centre of this cavern stood the man he had seen crossing the pit, his torch directed on the floor at his feet on an object that was swathed up in rugs. Holt could not see what it was at first, but he was soon to learn. The man with the torch was speaking.

'There's no harm coming to you if you're sensible,' he said in a low voice. 'If you're not, well — you know what happened to Dexon.' He paused significantly and then continued: 'Now you can eat your food. I expect you're hungry.'

He stooped, laid the torch on a nearby boulder, and then fumbling among the blankets straightened himself again. 'Here you are,' he said, taking a packet from his pocket and giving it into a hand that was stretched up. 'Wait a minute and I'll loosen the gag.' He bent once more and Holt heard a long sigh. 'Now eat, and be quick about it,' said the man. 'I want to get back.'

The figure in the blankets stirred and said something in so low a tone that the young American could not catch the words.

'Don't ask questions!' snapped the man. 'I shan't answer 'em, anyway. Eat your sandwiches and be quick about it. I want to get away, I tell you.'

Stanley Holt, the pain in his head forgotten, stared in stupefied astonishment. The bundle of rags was a human being, a prisoner. He had stumbled onto something with a vengeance. If he could only wait until the man had gone and release the person who lay on that heap of blankets, he might learn a lot more.

He tried to get a glimpse of the prisoner, but the other's figure blotted out the light of the torch and threw a deep shadow across the pile of blankets. There was a long silence while the unknown captive ate the food that had been brought and swallowed something from a flask.

'Now I'll make you all comfy again,' remarked the man when the meal was over, 'and clear off.'

He bent down and evidently replaced the gag and bound the wrists of his prisoner, for he said: 'This gag's only a precaution. You could shout yourself hoarse, but nobody would hear you,' and Holt caught a glimpse of a rope. 'Now I'm going,' said the man, picking up his torch. 'The next time I come will probably be the last.'

The young American thought he had better make himself scarce. He did not want to be caught by the other as he came out. He turned and began to creep cautiously back the way he had come, and then disaster overtook him. He kicked a loose stone, and the noise it made sounded deafening in that confined space.

The man evidently heard it, for from behind came a sharp exclamation. 'What's that? Who's there?' cried the rasping voice, and before Holt could evade it a beam of light focussed itself on him. He heard a frightened oath, and then the roar of a tremendous explosion. Something like a red-hot iron seared his left temple, and with the thunder of the pistol's report still echoing in his ears, he pitched forward on his face and lay motionless.

23

No Escape

He recovered consciousness to find himself lying on something remarkably hard, and in total darkness. There was a violent pain in his head, and one side of his face was stiff and uncomfortable. He tried to shift his position, but found that his hands had been bound tightly behind him and that his legs had been treated in a similar manner. A movement of his cramped fingers told him that he was lying on rough stone, and he concluded — rightly, as he discovered later — that he was in the big, cave-like chamber that had been cut out in the wall of the quarry.

The reason for the stiffness of his face troubled him for a long time, and then the explanation suddenly occurred to him. It was caused by the dried blood from the wound in his head where the bullet had grazed him. He would have given worlds for a drink, for his mouth and throat were parched and hot, and his thirst was in no way diminished by the gag that had been securely knotted about his head.

The silence of the place was intense. There was not a sound to be heard. A certain gruesome simile occurred to him and made him shiver a little. It was not unlike a tomb, this place — hewn out of the solid ground.

When the pain in his head had subsided a little, he tested his bonds, but his unknown captor had made a good job of securing him, and he quickly came to the conclusion that there was little hope of loosening them.

Panting from his exertions, he lay still, gazing into the blackness and trying to concoct some plan of escape. That he was in grave danger he was perfectly aware. Why he had not been killed at once was an extraordinary thing, for this man whom he had seen was undoubtedly connected with the murder of Felix Dexon and the other crimes, if he was not the prime mover in that sinister business.

Holt had not been able to see his face, but he had no doubt in his mind of that fact. Who the person was who was being kept prisoner he hadn't the least idea; could not even hazard a conjecture.

His thoughts turned to Farringdon, and he wondered what the reporter would think of his broken appointment. There was one ray of hope in that. Farringdon Street was a sensible fellow. Probably he would ring up his flat, discover he was not there, and institute further inquiries. The hope was only momentary, however. A second's thought convinced him how unlikely it was that the reporter would see anything in his absence to worry about. He would probably only conclude that for some reason of his own he had cut the dinner, and think no more about it. A more likely possibility was that someone would discover his car, and the discovery would reach the ears of the police. He became almost optimistic as this thought occurred to him.

In that pitch darkness time was non-existent. How long he lay staring into nothingness he could not have said, but presently he must have dropped off to sleep. Certainly there was a blank interval which he could not account for. When he awoke it might have been daylight or it might have been midnight for all he knew, and to the thirst had been added an intense hunger.

He shifted his aching limbs and tried to ease them from the soreness of the hard floor. As he turned over on his side with difficulty he heard a faint movement some distance away from him — a half-sigh, half-groan. It evidently came from his fellow-prisoner, and Holt wondered if by rolling himself over and over he could reach him. If he could he might be able to untie his bonds. It was worth the effort, anyhow.

He waited until that smothered sound came again, and then judging his direction as best he could, he began laboriously to put his plan into action. The rough floor hurt him, and his face was scratched and raw before he had gone more than a few yards. He set his teeth and stuck doggedly to his task. And then suddenly he was brought up with a thud against solid stone, and his heart sank. He had missed his objective, and either come up against a heap of stones or struck one of the walls of the cave. His disappointment was acute, but as he lay recovering his breath before making a second attempt, his fingers touched something that sent his hopes sky-high once more.

It was a sharp stone, so sharp that it cut the flesh of his palm, but he did not mind that. If only he could manoeuvre it into such a position that he could rub the cords of his wrist against it, it might be possible to cut through the strands. With a great deal of trouble he managed to get it between his fingers, and by twisting his hands, palms upward, he was able to touch the cords with the edge. It was a long and tedious business, for he could only work for a few seconds at a time, owing to the awkward position in which he had to hold his fingers. The pressure of the cords on his wrists stopped the circulation and numbed his hands so that he had to keep on stopping until it passed off.

At the end of what he concluded must have been nearly three hours, he had made very little headway. He took a rest and then started again, but to his despair he had barely begun before the stone slipped from his fingers. He groped about frantically, but it was a long time before he could find it and resume his labours. But he persevered, and at the end of what seemed eternity and was certainly several hours, had succeeded in almost severing one of the stout cords. The perspiration was streaming down his face when the strand gave and he felt the bonds at his wrists go loose.

With a sigh of relief he pulled the gag from his mouth and worked his stiff and aching jaws, and then set about undoing the ropes at his ankles. At last he was free, but his limbs were numb, and when he attempted to rise to his feet he found that he could not. He set about rubbing them to restore the circulation, and as life came back so did the pain get worse. For nearly ten minutes he writhed in agony as the released blood pumped through his veins. Presently, however, he felt better, and succeeded in getting to his feet. Feeling in his pocket, he found a box of matches and struck one. The feeble glow was lost in that cavernous place, but it gave sufficient light for him to be able to see his way about. He could dimly make out the heap of blankets and the motionless figure of the other prisoner, and with steps that were a trifle unsteady he made his way over to it.

He had reached the side of the captive when the match burnt down to his fingers and went out. He struck another. He was most anxious to see who this person was, but all that was visible was a heap of blankets. He bent down with the intention of pulling them away, and then:

'Keep quiet and put up your hands!'

The harsh voice came from the entrance of the cave, and swinging round he saw the figure of a man standing watching him, a long-barrelled pistol held menacingly in his hand. It was the man he had followed across the floor of the quarry.

Quick as thought he dropped the match, hoping in the sudden darkness that would follow that he would be able to take the newcomer by surprise. But the man was evidently prepared for this move, for almost coincident with the going out of the match flame a shaft of white light sprang from a torch and held Holt in its beam.

'Put up your hands, quick!' snarled the voice again, 'and don't try any funny business. If you do I shall shoot to kill.'

It was not a bluff. He was stating a fact, and Stanley Holt slowly raised his arms.

24

Street is Worried

Farringdon Street woke early on the morning following the dinner appointment with Stanley Holt at the Ritz-Carlton, and almost the first thing he did was to put through a call to the young American's flat. To his surprise the same voice that had spoken before answered, and told him that Holt had not returned since the previous morning.

'Do you mean that he hasn't been back all night?' asked the reporter.

'Yes, sir,' was the reply.

Farringdon frowned. 'Have you any idea where he is?' he demanded.

But the servant had no idea. He sounded a little worried and suggested that Farringdon should ring up Holt's office later and see if they could supply him with any information.

'I'm rather uneasy, sir,' he concluded.

'Mr. Holt's never stayed away before without letting me know.'

The reporter hung up the receiver and ate his breakfast thoughtfully. He was a trifle uneasy himself at this unaccountable disappearance of the American. Of course there might be nothing in it; Holt might have been suddenly called away on business. But in that event surely he would have left some message, or at least arranged to notify Farringdon and prevent him kicking his heels at the hotel for nothing. Perhaps he had done this, and the people at his office had forgotten to give the message.

At ten o'clock he telephoned Holt's office and was put through to his secretary, but she could offer no more information than the servant. Holt had left early on the previous afternoon in order, she thought, to keep a business appointment, but he had said nothing about being away for any length of time.

Farringdon's uneasiness increased. He felt there was something peculiar about the whole thing. Had something happened to Holt? Something that in an obscure way was connected with the Felix Dexon business? Holt was not actually mixed up in it, but he was a friend of the principal person concerned, and although the reporter could see no object in the person behind the business wishing him any harm, there might easily be one which he had overlooked. He made his way to Scotland Yard with the intention of talking the matter over with Hallick, but the inspector was not there. According to his sergeant, he had returned to the inn at Deneswood.

Farringdon went along to the offices of the *Morning Herald*, but there was little or nothing for him to do there, and presently he found himself in the neighbourhood of Bloomsbury, and called to inquire after the welfare of Lesley Thane.

She was not up, and he sent a message by Mrs. Williams asking if she would care to have lunch with him. Her reply disappointed him. She was still feeling very tired, and although she thanked him for his invitation, she hoped he would excuse her. Farringdon went back to Fleet Street and ate a solitary lunch in a snack bar.

He was sitting in the reporters' room of the *Morning Herald*, gloomily reading the morning edition of that enterprising paper, when a telephone call came through for him. It was from Hallick.

'That you, Street?' said the inspector. 'Listen. You know that friend of Miss Thane's who drove us down the other day, Stanley Holt?'

'Yes,' answered Farringdon, wondering what was coming.

'Well,' went on Hallick, 'his car has been discovered abandoned on a lonely road two miles outside of Deneswood. We rang up his office and his flat, but they haven't seen anything of him since yesterday. It looks to me as though something has happened to him.'

'I'll come down,' said the reporter promptly, and two hours later he was talking to the grave-faced Hallick in the little police station at Deneswood.

'It was one of the police patrols who found the car,' said the inspector, 'and he notified Blagdon, who remembered the name and immediately got in touch with me. There's no doubt about it being

Holt's car. There were some letters addressed to him in one of the door pockets. But there's no sign of Holt.'

'I wonder what the deuce could have happened to him,' muttered the reporter.

'I'm wondering that,' said Hallick. 'It looks bad to me. I've instituted a search of the neighbourhood in the vicinity of the place where the car was found abandoned, but nothing's been discovered yet.'

'Do you think his disappearance has anything to do with the Dexon business?' asked Farringdon.

Hallick nodded. 'Yes, I do,' he declared. 'It's my opinion that he's stumbled on something, and instead of notifying us, decided to do a little investigation on his own.'

'And fallen foul of the person responsible for the Dexon murder,' ended the reporter.

Again the inspector nodded. 'Yes,' he said gloomily. 'He was at Deneswood late yesterday afternoon.'

'How do you know that?' asked Street.

'One of my men saw him,' answered

Hallick. 'He was talking to that girl of Earnshaw's, and they drove away together.'

'Can't she give you any information?' inquired the reporter.

'I've seen her,' said Hallick, 'and if she's speaking the truth it doesn't help us much. She says she met Holt unexpectedly and he offered to drive her to the village. She accepted, and changed some books at the library there. After this they went out to the Anchor Hotel and had some tea, and he drove her back. When she left him it was a little after half past six. Nobody apparently set eyes on him after that.'

Farringdon scratched his chin irritably. 'I suppose this girl was speaking the truth?' he grunted, and to his surprise Hallick nodded.

'I'm sure she was,' he answered. 'I can pretty well tell when a person's lying, and she wasn't. She was terribly worried when she knew why I was questioning her, and I believe her worry was genuine.'

'Well, what are we going to do?' asked the reporter.

The inspector shrugged. 'What can we do?' he said. 'I'm having the locality searched, and the usual routine inquiries have been circulated. There's nothing else we can do. The fact that his car was found near Deneswood doesn't mean that Holt's in the locality. The abandoning of that on the road where it was found may have been a blind.'

'Did you see that fellow Thorpe?' asked Farririgdon as the thought suddenly occurred to him.

'Yes,' said Hallick. 'He's got nothing to do with it. He's a genuine fellow and was indignant at the thought that anyone had been using his cottage. Bit annoyed, too, that he should have been dragged all the way back from Bournemouth to answer questions.' He took a packet of cigarettes from his pocket, lit one, and blew out a cloud of smoke. 'The man I want to meet is this thin-faced fellow whom Miss Thane described,' he went on.

'Sam Gates,' said Farringdon, and Hallick pursed his lips.

'Perhaps,' he answered. 'Anyway, Sam Gates or Tom Smith, he's the fellow we want to get hold of, for he seems to be the prime mover in the business.'

271

'Are you staying in Deneswood tonight?' asked the reporter.

'Yes,' said Hallick. 'I've got a hunch that Deneswood is the spot which holds the secret of this business.'

'Have they got another room?' said Farringdon.

The inspector looked at him queerly. 'Thinking of staying?' he asked.

The reporter nodded. 'Yes, I think so. I feel the same as you do. I believe that if we ever find out the truth about Dexon we shall find it out here.'

How right he was proved. Before twenty-four hours had passed, the secret of Deneswood Valley was to be a secret no longer, for in those sylvan surroundings the final act of the drama was to be staged, in the same setting in which it had begun.

25

A Matter of Minutes

'Get over there against the wall!' said the man, still covering Holt with the pistol. 'And keep your hands well above your head.'

The young American obeyed reluctantly. He could do nothing else. Unarmed, it was useless to attempt to argue with an automatic. He backed slowly as the other advanced, and was able to see in the reflected light of the torch that the man wore some kind of a covering — it looked like a handkerchief — over his mouth and chin which effectually concealed his face. When he reached the wall the other stopped a yard away from him and surveyed him for a second in silence.

'So you managed to get free, did you?' he snarled. 'It was lucky I happened to come back in time.'

'Not for me,' remarked Holt coolly.

'No, not for you,' agreed the man, nodding. 'Certainly not for you.' He thought for a moment and then he went on: 'How did you come into this business? What brought you snooping round this place last night?'

'Curiosity,' said Holt coolly. 'I saw the light of your torch and followed you.'

'Oh, you followed me — I see.' The voice was low but harsh and rasping. 'Who are you?'

Holt thought rapidly before replying. This man, whoever he was, obviously did not know him. Should he tell him who he was? He decided not to.

'That's my business,' he answered.

The other uttered a savage imprecation. 'Is it!' he snapped. 'We'll see about that. Not that it matters very much who you are. You've seen too much for my safety and you'll have to take the consequences.'

There was a world of menace in his tone, and although the American remained outwardly calm, inwardly his heart sank. There was murder in that voice and in the eyes that were regarding him malignantly above the covering.

'Several people have had to take the consequences to ensure your safety,' he retorted. 'Felix Dexon was one. Feldon was another, and Sopley, too, unless I'm very much mistaken.'

The man started, and for a second was evidently taken aback.

'How do you know all this?' he hissed. 'How do you know it? Are you a 'busy'?'

'I'm the walking encyclopaedia of crime,' said Holt. 'I know everything.'

'Funny, aren't you?' snarled the other. 'You won't be laughing presently, I can tell you.'

'I'm not laughing now,' said Holt. 'I never laugh at my own jokes.'

'You'll laugh at mine,' was the retort. 'I'm going to show you the greatest joke you've ever seen.'

'You flatter yourself,' replied Holt. 'I've seen funnier people than you.'

His coolness rather disconcerted the man and he appeared to be uncertain how to take it. 'I'm serious,' he said after a slight pause. 'If you don't think I mean what I say you'd better think again.'

'Suppose, instead of wasting all this

time talking nonsense, you get on with it,' suggested Holt sharply. He was trying to work the other up into a rage. Men lose control of themselves when they lose their tempers, and he hoped that he might be able to take advantage of this fact and profit by it. But the masked man evidently had no intention of losing his temper, although it was only by a great effort that he controlled it.

'I will get on with it, as you call it, when I'm ready,' he said smoothly. 'I'm very anxious first of all to find out exactly who you are. When I caught you last night I was in too great a hurry to search you. That omission can be rectified now.'

Setting the torch on a heap of stone he came close to Holt, and ramming the muzzle of the pistol into his ribs, rapidly began to search his pockets. The miscellaneous collection of small change, keys, watch and other odds and ends he ignored, and it was not until he came upon a crumpled letter in the American's inside breast pocket that he showed any signs of interest at all. Then, as he read the name and address, he grunted.

'So that's who you are, is it?' he muttered. 'A friend of the girl's, eh?'

'That's who I am,' replied Holt sweetly. 'And now, if you'll tell me who you are, we shall have been properly introduced.'

'Friend of the Thane girl, eh?' murmured the other to himself, taking no notice of the remark. 'What were you doing down here?'

'Looking for fossils,' answered Holt promptly.

The other gripped his arm and shook him roughly. 'Answer my question!' he rasped. 'What were you doing here? Why did you come down? Are you working with the police?

'That's three questions,' retorted Holt. 'Don't you know the difference between singular and plural?'

The other gave him a savage thrust that sent him staggering against the stone wall. 'Keep a civil tongue in your head!' he hissed, almost choking with rage. 'I want to know how much you know.'

'It'll take too long to tell you that,' said Holt, his head spinning from the blow. 'I had a very good education.'

The other snarled something, and suddenly clubbing his pistol, he brought it down with all his force on Holt's unprotected scalp. Without even a groan the American slumped forward and slithered to the floor, where he lay in a crumpled heap.

'Now be funny!' growled the man, looking down at him, and then pocketing the pistol he took from his pocket a length of cord. Stooping, he proceeded to securely bind the unconscious form of his victim, and when he had finished he straightened up, wiping the perspiration from his forehead.

Picking up the torch, he went over and looked down at the inert figure of his other prisoner. There was no sound or movement, and with a grunt of satisfaction he came back to Holt. Laying the torch down again he hoisted the limp form of the American onto his shoulders, secured the light once more, and carrying him like a sack made his way over to the entrance to the cave. He negotiated the narrow passage and came out into the quarry. Here he switched off the torch and dropped it back into his pocket.

His most difficult task lay before him, for in order to carry out his plan he had to get the unconscious Holt up the almost sheer side of the pit. There was a point, however, where a landslide had made a rough kind of staircase, and by slow degrees he succeeded in his object. He was panting heavily and almost breathless by the time he reached the lip of the quarry with his heavy burden, and he had to lean against a pile of stones and rest before proceeding any further. After about five minutes, however, he had recovered sufficiently to continue. Picking Holt up once more, he staggered along down a steep declivity towards the open common.

There was scarcely any risk of his being seen, for this part was wild and deserted even in the full light of day, and at that time of night there was no chance of there being anybody about. Holt was no light-weight, and before he had gone two hundred yards the perspiration was streaming down his face under the covering handkerchief, and his muscles were aching. He had very little further to go, however, for ahead he could see the glimmer of the pool for which he was making. It lay, an uneven stretch of water, black and unpleasant-looking, its surface covered with green slime. He reached the edge, and laying his burden down began to search in the vicinity for stones with which to fill Holt's pockets.

The cool night air was bringing the American round, and he showed signs of movement as the man finished his task. It mattered very little now whether he recovered or not. It would be better for him if he did not, that was all. Once he had disappeared under the surface of that black water it would only be a question of minutes . . .

Bracing himself, he swung the body of the young American twice and hurled him out into the middle of the pool. There was a dull splash and the still surface of the stagnant water was broken by a succession of ripples.

For a moment the murderer stood looking into the darkness in the direction in which he had flung his victim. Then, turning, he vanished into the night.

26

Death at the Quarry

Farringdon Street stirred uneasily and sat up in bed with a jerk, staring about him into the darkness of the room. What had wakened him so suddenly he could not tell, but something had disturbed his sleep. He glanced across at the dim square of the window. It was still dark outside, and he listened, straining his ears, but no sound came to break the stillness of the night. Yet something had caused that sudden wakefulness.

He switched on the light and looked round the little hotel bedroom. He had carried out his intention of remaining at Deneswood, and had succeeded in securing a room at the inn in which Hallick was staying. Turning over on his side, he searched for and found the watch on the table by the bed. It was a little after two.

For perhaps ten minutes he sat

listening. Everything was still. And then, shivering slightly, for the night was cold, he lay down again and tried to sleep. He soon found that this was impossible; thoughts crowded into his brain and he became more wide awake than at mid-day. The uneasiness which he had felt ever since Holt's disappearance had increased a thousand fold, and for the hundredth time he vainly speculated as to what had happened to the young American.

He came to the conclusion that in his present state of his mind, sleep was impossible, and acting on an impulse, he got up and rapidly dressed himself. Anything was better than lying there tossing from side to side, his brain a chaos of disjointed thoughts, and he decided to go for a walk.

Passing the door of Hallick's room, it occurred to him to see if the inspector was awake, but with his hand on the handle a faint snore told him all he wanted to know, and he left him undisturbed. Hallick was to be disturbed before that night was over, but Farringdon did not know this then.

Making his way down the narrow staircase, he crossed the little lounge and unbolted the front door. The key was in the lock, and turning this gently he pulled the door open. The night was fine, and although there was a chill in the air, it was also inviting. He passed out into the cool darkness, closing the door softly behind him. Perhaps a brisk walk in the still night would tire him out.

He set off without any sense of direction, his thoughts still occupied with Stanley Holt's disappearance, and almost before he realised it he found himself passing the entrance to the private road that led to the Deneswood Estate. He paused for a second, debating with himself whether he should enter, and he concluded that it would be better not to. The plainclothes detectives were still on guard, and his appearance at that hour would lead to unnecessary questions.

He continued on up the road, and breasting the slope presently found himself walking along by the open common land that bordered the lip of the quarry. He was still feeling very wide awake, and although he had already come a considerable distance, he made up his mind to continue.

It was very still and peaceful, and his thoughts turned to Lesley Thane. Even to himself he refused to admit his feelings for the girl. There was an insurmountable barrier that rendered any such feelings hopeless: the barrier of Felix Dexon's wealth. Lesley Thane was now an heiress and beyond the reach of a mere reporter.

He had turned off the road and was making his way across the common, moving slowly over the uneven ground. She would probably return to America when all the excitement had died down, and that would be the last he would see of her. Well, it was much the best way . . .

He stopped suddenly. Somewhere in the darkness ahead of him he had heard a sound — the splash of water.

He peered in the direction of the noise and made out a dark figure running, about a hundred yards away. His thoughts connected the hurrying man with the splash he had heard, and he started to give chase. The other was moving at a fast pace, and the reporter had just increased his when a thin cry from behind him brought him to a sudden halt.

He remembered the sound of that dull splash. There must be water near at hand, perhaps a pond or a river, and the runner had thrown someone in.

The thin cry was repeated, and Farringdon could distinguish the word, 'Help!'

He swung round and hurried towards the place from whence the feeble cry had come, and as he ran he dragged a torch from his pocket, sending a bright beam dancing before him to guide his steps. The cries were not repeated, but now, in the white light of the torch, he could see the black expanse of a stretch of water, its surface agitated as something struggled below its surface. Without pausing for an instant, Farringdon flung aside the torch, tore off his coat, and the next moment was wading into the pond, searching frantically for the cause of those sinister ripples.

The bottom shelved deeply, and a few yards away from the edge he found it was too deep to stand upright and had to swim. He had marked the spot in his mind from whence the ripples emanated, and, reaching this, he dived, feeling about with his hands. They touched something cold and wet . . . flesh . . .

He managed to get a grip of clothing and tugged. Something moved heavily, but he could not raise it. He knew that what he was holding was a human form, but heavier than any human form should be.

Tugging, struggling and gasping, he exerted all his strength, and by slow degrees managed to drag the thing in the pond into the shallows. Three minutes later he had got his heavy, soaking burden onto firm ground, and retrieving his torch, he threw the light onto the face of the man he had rescued. It was Stanley Holt!

* * *

Stanley Holt, clad in a sketchy attire that consisted of Hallick's pyjamas and a dressing gown of Farringdon's, gulped the hot whisky that the sleepy landlord at the inn had hurriedly prepared, and pulled his chair closer to the newly lit fire in the lounge. He had been unconscious when the reporter had dragged him out of the pool which had so nearly been his grave, but Farringdon had succeeded in bringing him round and had managed to get him back to the inn. Hallick had been awakened and told of the adventure, and when the landlord had been roused and the fire lighted, Holt had sufficiently recovered from his terrible experience to give them a brief account of his discovery in the quarry.

'The most important question we have to answer,' said Hallick thoughtfully, 'is, who is this other prisoner?'

'That's been puzzling me,' said Holt.

'It's a question that's easily settled,' remarked Farringdon. 'Let's go to the quarry now and find out.'

'That's a good idea of yours, Street,' agreed Hallick, rising to his feet.

'I wish I could come with you,' said the American, looking ruefully at his ill-fitting pyjamas and dressing gown, 'but I've got no clothes.'

'I don't think you ought to come even if you had, Mr. Holt,' said the inspector. 'You've been through quite enough. If you take my advice, you'll slip along to my room and have a good rest.'

Holt, who was so tired that he could scarcely keep his eyes open, required very little persuading to take this advice, and when they had seen him comfortably ensconced in Hallick's bed, they left the inn.

The sky was lightening in the east as they set out for the quarry, and the chill of dawn was in the air, but they were both too busy with their thoughts to feel the cold wind that had sprung up and was blowing in fitful gusts across the expanse of common. Who was the person who was being kept in that cave in the quarry? They discussed the matter as they strolled along, but could come to no satisfactory solution.

They reached the lip of the quarry and began to seek for an easy way down. They found the place where the masked man had laboriously carried up the unconscious body of Holt, and began to climb down. Reaching the bottom, they set off towards the mass of rocks that partially masked the entrance to the cave and which Farringdon would always associate with that never-to-be-forgotten morning when he and Blagdon had discovered the prison house of Felix Dexon.

'We'll have to be careful,' muttered Hallick as they entered the gloomy opening, 'in case there's anybody lurking about in here.'

They listened, but there was no sound, and cautiously they advanced along the passage until they came to the dividing of the ways. Taking the left-hand gallery, they rounded the bend and came to the point where the passage broadened into the cave-like chamber. Here they stopped again, but all was silent. Not a sound broke the intense stillness. Switching on the light of the torch he carried, Hallick stepped boldly forward, spraying it from side to side.

They saw the dark heap of rugs in the middle of the floor and went over curiously. 'Now let's see who this mysterious person is,' grunted Hallick, pulling off the blankets which covered the motionless form.

Farringdon's cry of horror drowned the inspector's oath. For the thing that the blanket had covered was the dead body of Harold Earnshaw. He had died as Mr. Sopley had died, and the blood from the wound in his throat had soaked into the blankets on which he lay.

27

The Man Responsible

Hallick looked down at the dead man, his face set and grim.

'Is he quite dead?' whispered Farringdon, and the inspector nodded.

'Quite,' he answered sternly. 'He couldn't have lived very long with a wound like that.' He knelt beside the body and touched one of the hands. The flesh was still warm. 'He wasn't killed so very long ago, either,' he muttered. 'The blood's still wet. Surely he couldn't have been the prisoner whom Holt saw. We should have heard if he'd disappeared.'

'Then they must have succeeded in getting the other person away,' said the reporter a little obviously, as he realized as soon as the words had left his lips.

'Probably discovered that their plan to kill Holt had failed,' grunted Hallick as he rose to his feet. 'The question is, how did

Earnshaw get here?'

'That's not the only question,' answered Farringdon wearily. 'There are dozens of questions. I can think of enough to fill a large-sized notebook.'

'So could I,' growled Hallick, rubbing his chin. 'Well, I suppose we'd better notify Blagdon of this.'

'I'll go, if you like,' offered the reporter.

'I'd be glad if you would,' said Hallick. 'One of us certainly ought to stay on guard. Tell him to bring a doctor and a stretcher.'

Farringdon nodded and left the underground cave, scrambled up the side of the quarry, and set off almost at a run for the little police station at Deneswood. As he reached the entrance, to his surprise, Blagdon came out. The local man had evidently dressed himself hurriedly and looked sleepy-eyed and dishevelled.

'Hello!' he said as he caught sight of Street. 'How did you know anything about it?' The reporter was rather taken aback.

'I made the discovery with Hallick,' he said. 'Who told you?'

'You made the discovery with Hallick?'

echoed Blagdon in blank astonishment. 'But they notified no one but me! The telephone message came through twenty minutes ago to the police station, and the sergeant on duty sent to wake me up — '

'Twenty minutes ago!' echoed Farringdon. 'Why — we've only just found the body — '

'Body?' Blagdon's eyes opened wide. 'What body? I've heard nothing about that. All I was told was that someone had broken in — '

'I think we're talking at cross purposes,' said the reporter, interrupting him. 'I'm referring to the murder of Harold Earnshaw. Hallick and I discovered his body in that cave at the quarry a few minutes ago.'

'I don't know anything about that,' said the inspector quickly. 'I'm talking about an attempted burglary at Blessington's. Has there been another murder then?'

Rapidly, Farringdon told him of the happenings of the night.

'This is more serious than Blessington's burglary,' said Blagdon when he had finished. 'Just a minute. I'll get my sergeant to ring up the police doctor. I think I'd better go along to the quarry first. I'll send up to Blessington's and tell them to hang on until I can get there.'

'I'll go if you like,' said the reporter, and Blagdon accepted the offer gratefully. Most of his men were out on patrol and he was glad of Farringdon's help. He re-entered the police station and Farringdon hurried away on his errand.

Farringdon found the house brilliantly lit and one of the plainclothes officers on guard at the front door. To him he rapidly explained the situation and went in to interview Mr. Blessington. He found that gentleman only partially dressed, being clad in a pyjama jacket and a pair of trousers, over which he wore an ornate, many-hued dressing gown. His head was still bandaged, and he received Farringdon in his sumptuously furnished library which, unlike that at Feldon's house, contained more books than anything else.

'A terrible business, Mr. Street,' he said tragically. 'I appear to be surrounded by robbery and death.'

'What happened?' asked the reporter briefly.

Mr. Blessington took a sip of whisky from the glass by his side. 'My butler made the discovery,' he said, 'and woke me. Somebody broke in by the French windows in the drawing room, and Oliver, my man, heard him and came down. Luckily he frightened him away before any serious damage could be done. But in the state of my nerves the shock has been irreparable. I am naturally of a rather nervous disposition' — he smiled a trifle apologetically — 'and I must say that all these incidents, happening one on top of another, are having a serious effect on my health. I shall really have, much as I dislike the thought, to go away in order to recuperate.' He took another drink from his glass and Farringdon wondered what he would say when he learned of the tragic fate of Earnshaw. 'I instructed Oliver,' he went on, 'to phone the police. It was an extremely unpleasant experience, and most alarming.'

'I suppose,' said the reporter, 'you didn't see what this man was like?'

Mr. Blessington shook his large head. 'I never saw him at all,' he replied. 'But I asked my butler the same question and he could offer no description. This atmosphere of violence is very dreadful, Mr. Street,' said the stout man sorrowfully. 'The pleasant, peaceful stream of life that we have always experienced here has during the past few weeks been rudely shattered, I fear.'

'Completely broken, I should say,' said the reporter, am then suddenly: 'Another murder was committed tonight.'

Mr. Blessington looked at him in horror. 'Good heavens!' he exclaimed. 'Who — who is the latest — er — victim?'

'Mr. Earnshaw,' answered Farringdon. 'He was stabbed in the throat at the quarry some time during the past hour and a half.'

'But this is terrible! Dear me! Dreadful!' said the stout man in a shocked voice. 'Earnshaw! Charming man, charming man.'

'Delightful!' said the reporter dryly. 'The police are under the impression that he was in league with the murderer.'

Mr. Blessington gasped like a newly landed fish. 'In league? Good gracious! You astonish me. Why, then, was he killed?'

'Because we think he knew too much,'

replied Farringdon, and he gave the stout proprietor of Deneswood Valley an account of what had happened at the quarry.

'Incredible!' cried Mr. Blessington in horror. 'Incredible! It is almost beyond belief that so much wickedness could exist. Who can be at the bottom of this dreadful business? Have you any suspicion? It is a very terrible thought that this fiend — this murderer — is living in our midst. One will never feel safe until he is apprehended. I hope that the police will not rest until he is under lock and key.'

'I can assure you, Mr. Blessington,' replied the reporter a little absently, 'that everything will be done that is possible.' He leaned forward. 'May I have one of your cigars? I'm afraid I've run out of cigarettes.'

'My dear sir, certainly,' said Mr. Blessington, and he pushed forward a box that stood on the table at his elbow. 'Really, you must forgive me for not having offered you one before, but the excitement of — er — of the night, you know, and — er — '

'Please don't apologise,' said Street hurriedly. 'I quite understand.' He reached out a long arm and helped himself to one of the brown cylinders. In withdrawing his arm his sleeve caught on the edge of the box and it toppled off the table and fell on the floor, scattering its contents on the carpet.

'I'm terribly sorry,' he apologised. 'Most clumsy of me.' He was on his knees in an instant and began picking up the cigars hastily. 'It was my sleeve button . . . '

'It is my turn to say please don't apologise,' said Mr. Blessington with a smile, and then, as the reporter replaced the box on the table and sat down, 'Can I offer you any — er — refreshment?'

Farringdon shook his head. 'No, thank you,' he replied. 'By the way, Mr. Blessington, you haven't been wounded at all, have you?'

'Wounded?' said his host, his eyebrows going up in surprise. 'Not — er — not recently. I was — er — rather badly hurt when that disgusting attack was made on me the other night, but I'm thankful to say that I have almost completely recovered.'

'That's curious,' said Farringdon, and there was a note in his voice that caused the other to look at him sharply.

'Why is it curious?' he inquired. 'Surely — '

'I'll tell you why it's curious!' snapped the reporter suddenly. 'It's curious because although you have not recently been wounded, the welt of your right-hand boot is sodden with blood!'

Mr. Blessington made a movement forward, but the hand that Farringdon withdrew from his pocket held a pistol, and the muzzle covered him unwaveringly. 'You've made a mistake. Your first,' said the reporter grimly. 'You forgot to change your boots after you came from the quarry, and one of them is still covered with the blood of Harold Earnshaw. A slight mistake, but a fatal one for you. I saw the gleam of it in the light, and in order to make quite sure, I upset those cigars so that I could get a closer look. Put up your hands, Mr. Blessington, or Sam Gates, or whatever your real name is, and keep them up. If you try to reach that pistol in your pocket I'll blow the top of your head off!'

28

The Secret of Deneswood

Mr. Blessington slowly raised a pair of podgy hands and his large face wore an expression of amazed bewilderment. 'You're making a very great mistake, Mr. Street,' he said, and though he strove to speak calmly there was a slight shake in his voice. 'A very great mistake indeed. You will get into serious trouble over this.'

'I'll take the risk!' snapped Farringdon. 'It's useless bluffing, Mr. Blessington. You can't explain away that blood on your boot.'

'My dear man' — there was something very like a sneer in the slow, measured voice — 'that is not sufficient proof. No jury would regard that as sufficient proof. I can't at the moment account for its presence, but I dare say there is a very simple explanation.'

'There is,' retorted the reporter. 'The

explanation I have already given you. Besides that, I think the biggest proof of all will be found in this house.'

'What do you mean?' Blessington's face changed and a flicker of fear showed for a second in his eyes.

'I mean the person you were keeping prisoner at the quarry,' replied Farringdon sharply. 'That person is in this house now, somewhere. When you discovered that the attempt to kill Holt had failed you hurried the person you were keeping captive away from the cave and brought him here, and then in case there was a chance that you might be suspected you staged your little comedy of the attempted burglary. It was all very clever, but you really should have put on a different pair of boots.'

He was bluffing, but the expression on the stout man's face justified the bluff. Blessington looked at him from beneath drooping lids which gave to his face a new meaning — a savage and ruthless expression. His lips moved soundlessly and his fat cheeks had gone a curious grey.

'You're very clever, aren't you?' he said. 'But you haven't got me yet.'

'Then you admit that you have been responsible for all these crimes?' cut in the reporter quickly.

The other shook his head. 'I admit nothing!' he snarled, and then laughed — a mirthless laugh — loud and long. 'You fool! D'you think I can be caught as easily as this?'

Something — a fleeting expression — warned Farringdon of danger. At the same moment a hard, cold ring ground into the back of his neck and a hand reached over his shoulder and wrenched his pistol from his grasp.

'You keep still,' grunted a voice from behind him. 'Don't move or it will be the worse for you.'

'That's right, Oliver, keep him quiet,' said Blessington, getting heavily to his feet. 'You fool!' he said again, thrusting his big face close to Farringdon. 'There's a bell push let into the floor under my desk, concealed by the carpet. It was put there in case of just such an emergency as this. When that's rung Oliver knows that it's urgent. It is the first time I've had occasion to use it though. That white-livered lot in the valley wouldn't dare to try anything, except Earnshaw, and he's suffered for his temerity.'

It was not until later that Farringdon understood the meaning of his words. 'What do you think you can do?' he said calmly. 'There's a police officer outside the door of this house, and a word from him will bring others to his assistance. You can't get away. The best thing you can do, Blessington, is to give in. Tell this crook butler of yours to take that damn thing away from my neck, and be sensible.'

'Can't get away, can't I?' snarled the other furiously. 'Perhaps I can't, but I can try, and whatever I do can't make any difference. I'll be hanged anyway — if I'm caught.' He pulled an automatic from the pocket of his dressing gown and covered Street. 'Go down to the door!' he snapped to the man Oliver, 'and ask that detective to come up. Wait until he's inside the hall and then get him. Don't shoot — cosh him. We don't want 'em to hear any sound outside if we can help it.'

The cold pressure at the back of the reporter's neck was removed. 'All right,' muttered Oliver, and he departed noiselessly, his feet making no sound on the thick carpet.

'Where's that other fellow — the one who came prowling round the quarry? What's his name — Holt?' asked Blessington when they were alone.

'He's at the inn,' answered the reporter. 'You're a fool, Blessington, to think you can get away. Blagdon and Hallick will be here at any moment.'

The stout man chuckled. 'The more the merrier,' he said. 'Can't get away, eh? We'll see about that, Mr. Cocksure Street. Once I've silenced you and that fool detective I don't think anybody's going to stop me.'

Farringdon's lips curled at the corners. 'You're like all the rest,' he sneered. 'Full of your own importance. Vanity's your trouble, Blessington, and over ninety per cent of the criminals I've come up against have suffered from the same disease.'

'Well, we'll see,' snarled the other, but his fat face flushed at the taunting words.

'I'm in a tight corner, I'll admit, but I think I can see a way out.'

'There's nothing like being optimistic,' said the reporter, and although he spoke coolly his brain was working rapidly to find a way of turning the tables. 'I suppose you've forgotten that the place is surrounded by detectives?'

'I've forgotten nothing,' answered Blessington. 'In spite of that I think I shall succeed in getting away. Well?' He added the last word in a changed tone, but without shifting his eyes from Farringdon.

'I got him all right.' Oliver had evidently returned. 'He's lying all nice and comfy in the hall.'

'Good!' Blessington nodded his satisfaction. 'Now you' — he jerked his pistol at the reporter — 'get up and walk.'

'Why don't you give up this nonsense,' said Farringdon, without moving. 'You're only putting off the evil day. You're bound to be caught in the end. Why don't you give in and go quietly?'

'I see. Just say, 'It's a fair cop,' like a little sneak-thief caught 'dipping' a girl's handbag,' sneered the fat man. 'I'm not

305

like that, Street. I've played for big stakes all my life, and I'll go on playing for 'em until — '

'Until they drop you at the end of a rope,' cut in Farringdon quickly. 'Doesn't seem worth all the trouble, does it, Blessington?'

'I'm not at the end of a rope yet,' breathed Blessington. 'Not even in the death-house. I'm not going to waste any more time listening to your talk. Go on, get up and walk.'

Farringdon shrugged and rose slowly. He kept his eyes fixed on the pistol in the other's hand, and if there had been the slightest possible chance he would have risked a dash for it, but Blessington kept it steadily pointed at him, and his hand was as steady as a rock. Whatever he might be, the reporter felt a certain grudging admiration for his nerve. He was a fighter, a man who refused to admit that he was beaten.

'Come on, get a move on,' he ordered, and Farringdon was forced out into the corridor and down the stairs. 'And hurry yourself,' went on the fat man. 'You

— Oliver. Go and fetch that 'busy' and bring him down to the cellar.'

Oliver nodded and hurried on ahead. As they reached the dimly lighted hall Farringdon saw him stoop, pick up the unconscious figure of the detective and sling it over his shoulders like a sack of potatoes. Blessington directed the reporter down a passage at the far end of the hall, and waited while Oliver unlocked a heavy door on the right. A rush of cold, damp-smelling air came up from the open doorway to greet Farringdon's nostrils.

'There's a flight of steps beyond,' said Blessington. 'Down you go.'

'Where does this lead to?' asked Farringdon as he crossed the dark threshold.

'You'll see!' was the retort.

The fat man pressed a switch beside the doorway and a yellow gleam of light split the darkness in front. The reporter saw that the steps led down to a low-roofed cellar, the walls, floor and ceiling of which were of stone.

'This is where I first thought of keeping Dexon,' remarked Blessington. 'Sound-proof — there's an inner cellar with a steel door. You'll see it in a moment.'

Farringdon saw it in less than a moment. It was about halfway along the main cellar wall and fitted into a niche. Oliver, at a word from Blessington, laid down the unconscious form of the plainclothes man and took the revolver from his master's hand.

'Keep him covered,' said the fat man with a chuckle. He felt in his pocket, took from it a bunch of keys, and fitted one to the lock of the steel door. A twist of the wrist and a pull, and the heavy, safe-like door swung open.

'In with the 'busy',' growled Blessington, taking back the pistol from Oliver's hand, and the man picked up the detective and swung him through the aperture.

Farringdon heard a faint, startled cry. It was a girl's voice, and then he received a shattering blow in the back that sent him staggering into the cell-like room, and before he could recover his balance the steel door clanged shut behind him.

'Who is it? Who's there?' asked a frightened voice, and the reporter uttered an exclamation of astonishment, for it was the voice of Lesley Thane!

29

The End of Sam Gates

Ambrose Blessington, or Sam Gates, to give him his real name, gave a gasp of relief and mopped his damp forehead with a silk handkerchief. The strain of the last quarter of an hour had been terrific. 'Thank God that's over!' he breathed. 'Come on, we've still a lot to do.'

'You're right, as far as it goes,' grunted Oliver, 'but I don't see what you're going to do now. It's alive with detectives outside. 'ow d'you think you're going to dodge em?'

'Quite easily, I hope,' replied the fat man, leading the way back to the hall. 'Lock that door to the cellar and then go and stand by the front door and don't let anyone in. If any of those cursed 'busies' call, get rid of them. Cosh 'em if necessary, but don't let 'em in. Understand?'

'I'll do my best,' growled Oliver. 'But I

can't deal with the 'ole blooming police force.'

'You're not asked to,' snarled Blessington. 'All I want is to gain a few minutes' time.'

He hurried upstairs, taking the broad treads two at a time. Going into his bedroom, he pulled the heavy curtains across the window and switched on the light. Removing his dressing gown, he went over to the wardrobe and collected a dark blue lounge suit. With remarkable celerity he stripped and redressed in the other suit. Over this he put his dressing gown and thrust a cap into one of the pockets. Then, switching out the light, he went into his study. Crossing to the large safe that stood against the wall, he twisted the combination until it spelt the word 'black' and pulled open the door. He ignored the orderly heaps of letters and documents, and opening a steel drawer removed a large wad of high-denomination notes which he thrust into his pocket. A couple of fresh clips of cartridges for his pistol, taken from his desk, completed his preparations. He poured himself out a stiff whisky and drank it neat, then leaving the lights burning made his way down to the hall.

Oliver was still waiting on guard by the front door. 'Now follow me,' whispered Blessington.

'What you going to do?' demanded the butler. 'Going by the passage?'

'No, you fool!' snapped the fat man. 'The other end of that comes out by the quarry, and we'd be almost certain to be seen.'

'Listen!' gasped the butler, grasping his master by the arm.

Blessington listened. The sound of a car coming to a halt outside in the drive reached his ears. A curse left his lips and he stiffened.

'That's the police,' whispered Oliver, his face white with fear.

'Stay there,' hissed the fat man, and slipping into the dining room he peered cautiously through the window.

A few yards away the police car had come to a halt. He saw Blagdon get out, leaving the constable who had been driving in the car. The inspector moved towards the porch, and Blessington left his point of vantage and returned to the hall. An idea had occurred to him. A daring scheme, but possessing many advantages. 'It's Blagdon,' he whispered.

'Hell!' said his servant, and then in alarm as his master laid a hand on the catch. 'What are you going to do? Are you mad?'

'No, you fool! Be quiet!' hissed the fat man, opening the door. 'Come in, Inspector,' he greeted Blagdon genially as he mounted the steps. 'Come in. Mr. Street is here and he's made an important discovery. He wants to see you.'

The unsuspecting Blagdon crossed the threshold. 'I hear you've been having trouble here, Mr. Blessington,' he said as the stout man closed the door.

'I'm afraid we have,' said Blessington softly, and the butt of his revolver came down with all its force on the back of the inspector's neck. 'Catch him!' he snarled as the burly figure crumpled, and Oliver sprang forward and took the weight of the unconscious police official. 'Get some rope and tie him up,' said Blessington, removing his dressing gown, 'and then come back here. Be quick.'

Oliver hastened to obey. He disappeared in the direction of the kitchen and presently returned with a length of clothes-line. With this he hastily bound Blagdon's wrists and ankles.

'Pull him into the dining room,' ordered Blessington, when he had finished, and when this had been done he once more opened the front door. 'The inspector wants you, officer,' he said mildly to the constable seated at the wheel of the police car. 'Will you come in?'

The man got down, crossed the intervening strip of gravel and ascended the steps.

'He's in the dining room,' said Mr. Blessington, and as the policeman passed him his clenched fist shot out and caught him on the point of the jaw. With a smothered cry the constable staggered, and in that second Blessington acted. With a lightning spring he was down the steps and beside the police car. Another second and he had sprung up behind the steering wheel and was thrusting frantically at the self-starter pedal. The engine jarred into life just as

Oliver, dazed with the rapidity with which it had all happened, came flying up.

'Here, wait for me, Guv'nor!' he shouted, springing onto the running-board as the car began to move.

Blessington swept round a powerful arm and the butler went sprawling onto the gravel of the drive. 'You can go to the devil!' he snapped, pressing hard on the accelerator.

Like a living thing the car leaped forward and shot down the drive with the rapidity of a bullet. Blessington heard a shout behind him and the crack of an automatic as he was seen by one of the plainclothes men, but the bullet went wide. He took the turning out of the private road almost on two wheels, and skidded into the main thoroughfare, wrenching the wheel hard over to swing the radiator towards the open country.

It was light now, and a pale sun was flooding the road ahead — a long, deserted stretch that passed the lip of the quarry. The car slowed appreciably as it breasted the slope, but Blessington cared little for that. He had got away! It was cursed ill luck that he had had to make a break for it just when success was in his grasp. That fatal mistake of not changing his boots after he had come back from the quarry. But for that, Farringdon Street would never have become suspicious. Well, anyway, he'd got away.

He reached the top of the rise and felt the car bound forward with redoubled speed as it came onto the flat, and then ahead he saw a lorry approaching. At the same instant a man came running unevenly across the tract of common land. It was Hallick, and he stared in astonishment as he caught sight of the speeding police car with Blessington at the wheel.

Almost coincident with the sight, his mind supplied the reason. He was close to the approaching lorry, and he shouted to the driver. 'Turn your lorry across the road!' he cried. 'I'm a police officer. Block the road and stop that car!'

For an instant the lorry driver hesitated, and then the authority in the voice took effect. He slowed, twisted the wheel, and the huge, lumbering machine swerved and stopped, completely blocking the narrow thoroughfare. Blessington saw the man-oeuvre, cursed, wrenched at the wheel of the car, and swung off the road onto the uneven common land, bumping and jolting as he kept his foot hard down on the accelerator. He heard a report like a pistol shot and the wheel twisted loosely under his hand. The car zigzagged spasmodically, its steering out of control. He heard a voice scream frantically. 'Look out, man! The quarry!'

He recognised his danger, and tried desperately to pull the car up. But he was too late! The radiator dropped at an appalling angle. For a second or two the machine hovered uncertainly on the lip of the pit, and then went crashing to the bottom, turning over and over as it fell . . .

When Hallick, some minutes later, succeeded in scrambling down by way of the landslide and made his way to the wreck of the machine, Blessington was stone dead. He was lying half under the heavy car, a horrible, sprawling shape with a thin trickle of blood running sluggishly from the corner of his open mouth.

30

The Motto of America

A taxi drew up outside the house of the ex-policeman Williams in Bloomsbury, and Farringdon Street alighted, followed by Inspector Hallick.

'Wait,' said the reporter to the driver, and ascending the steps he rang the bell.

Mrs. Williams answered the door and smiled as she recognised the visitor. 'You want to see Miss Thane, sir?' she asked, and the reporter nodded. She disappeared up the stairs, after ushering them into the hall, and presently the girl came down.

'How are you, Mr. Street?' she greeted him. 'You wish to see me?'

Before the reporter could reply, Hallick stepped forward. I wish to see you,' he said sternly. 'The game's up, Mrs. Canning. You'd better come quietly.'

'I — I don't know what you mean,' she gasped. 'My name is Thane — '

'Since when?' broke in Hallick roughly. 'It's no good. Blessington's accomplice, Oliver, has squealed, and we know all about you. There's no need to make a fuss if you come quietly.'

The trapped woman looked from one to the other, oblivious of the horrified stare of Mrs. Williams.

'All right, I'll come,' she whispered softly, and taking her arm Hallick led her to the waiting cab.

The deception had been discovered immediately when Farringdon had found the real Lesley Thane, a prisoner in the cellar in which Blessington had thrust him on the morning of his attempted getaway. She had been the prisoner in the quarry whom Holt had seen, and had never returned to Bloomsbury at all. The story the false Lesley Thane had put up about her escape from the cottage near Godalming had been a tissue of lies, invented and drilled into her by Blessington himself. Her description of the thin man had existed only in Blessington's imagination and had been introduced to lead the police on a false trail. The cottage owned by the indignant Mr. Thorpe had been carefully prepared for the arrival of the police and the ambush laid in the hope that Hallick would fall into the trap, which he had almost done.

It had been one of the most ingenious schemes planned by the fertile brain of Sam Gates, and might very easily have been successful. Few people in England knew Lesley Thane sufficiently to challenge the imposture, and with the girl a prisoner, any letters or documents could have been written or signed by her and passed on to her double. It was very unlikely that any suspicion would have been aroused, particularly as the supposed injury to her hand would have prevented her signing anything on the spot. She could always have made the excuse that she wished to consider any documents before attaching her signature, and taken them away to be signed by the real Lesley Thane. If the scheme had not been exploded, Felix Dexon's fortune would have undoubtedly continued to pour into the coffers of the ingenious Sam Gates.

The use of the quarry in which to

imprison Lesley Thane after her abduction from the house in Bloomsbury had been another of his clever schemes. He had concluded, and rightly, that the place having once been searched by the police after Felix Dexon had succeeded in making his escape, would be the safest hiding place. No one would imagine for an instant that the same place would be used again for the same purpose.

'That man was one of the cleverest criminals I've ever come up against,' was Hallick's comment when the tearful Mrs. Canning had been lodged safely in Cannon Row. 'And we've only discovered a part of his cleverness. The rest has still to come out.'

It was two days later before it did, when the contents of the house at Deneswood Valley had been carefully examined and certain documents that had been kept in a box at the Safe Deposit in Chancery Lane were brought to light. And then they learned the real secret of the Deneswood Estate.

Blessington, or to give him his real name, Sam Gates, had at one time been a solicitor. He had specialised in cases that, to put it mildly, could not be investigated too closely, and had eventually been struck off the Rolls. During the period of his legal operations, however, he had acquired a considerable amount of money and also a lot of out-of-the-way information that later was to prove the basis of one of the most ingenious schemes in the history of crime.

He conceived and built the Deneswood Valley Estate, and then he went systematically to work to find suitable tenants, and they had to be suitable in two ways. They had to be rich, and they also had to have something criminal in their past lives that was known to Gates and which he could hold over them and use as a means of extorting blackmail. That, in a nutshell, was the secret of the valley. Every resident was a man who, in the acquiring of his wealth, had overstepped the law and against whom Gates held evidence that could send him to prison. He forced them to live in the valley, and it was a very paying scheme, for his blackmail was levied in the form of rent and was therefore untraceable.

From his books Hallick discovered that Sopley had been paying two thousand a year for his house, and Feldon three, and the others in proportion to their income. So cleverly had Gates gone to work that those paying the largest sums had the larger houses, so that had anyone at any time questioned such exorbitant charges it was quite easy to reply that the valley was a very select community arid therefore if people wished to live there and enjoy its facilities they had to pay for it. Gates waxed fat and rich, but he foresaw his greatest danger and guarded against it. It was quite possible that one of his victims might kick against being squeezed so regularly and for such a large sum and try and remove the man who held them at his mercy. In order to safeguard himself against attacks, Gates rendered any such course futile by letting it be known that full particulars regarding each individual crime had been deposited with his solicitors in a sealed envelope with instructions to forward it to the police in the event of his death. This rendered him perfectly safe, or so he thought, until he went too far in the case of Harold Earnshaw.

He had conceived a desire to marry Pamela and had used his hold on her father to force him to bring about this end. Earnshaw had kicked. He had determined to break the shackles which Gates had wound about him. The attack on the golf course was his first attempt; the second he had made on the night when Gates and Oliver had been in the act of removing Lesley Thane from the quarry to the house.

When Blessington had built the estate he had had a passage constructed from the cellar of his own house to a golf hut near the quarry. By this means it was possible for him to visit Felix Dexon in his prison, and, later, to come and go while the estate was being watched by the men whom Hallick had put on guard. Earnshaw had been decoyed into the quarry on the pretext of talking matters over, and there killed.

Gates's schemes would have gone well but for the greediness which proved his undoing. He heard about Felix Dexon from Feldon, and conceived the idea of getting his hands on Dexon's money. He forced Feldon to decoy Dexon down to the valley and then imprisoned him in the quarry, torturing him until he agreed to write the letters received by the lawyers and the receipts for the money they forwarded.

His scheme worked. Sopley and Earnshaw had been forced to help him in the conspiracy, and then, like a bolt from the blue, came Lew Miller, an old associate of Gates's, who had just come out of prison. He had succeeded in tracing Gates to the valley, but didn't know that his name was now Blessington. The man had changed beyond recognition, for good living and prosperity had fattened him. Besides which, Gates, in the old days when Miller had known him, had worn a moustache.

Miller, however, was a danger, and at any time he might discover that Gates was Blessington; and he drank, and men who drank also talked. Gates considered the matter, and when Miller, more drunk than he had been in the afternoon, came back to the valley that night, he made sure of his silence forever. He had followed

Farringdon when the reporter had called to see Feldon and listened under the window. He had heard Feldon make his midnight appointment with the reporter and had taken the only step possible to prevent Feldon giving the game away. He had killed him, taking the contents of the safe in case Feldon had left behind anything that incriminated him in writing.

The biggest shock of his career had been the arrival of the escaped Felix Dexon at Feldon's house. A word from him and the trap yawned at his feet. He made sure that word was never uttered. He was near the light switch and he acted promptly. After shooting Dexon he put the revolver on the top of the clock, where later it had been found. His greatest touch of genius, however, undoubtedly lay in his abduction of Lesley Thane, and the substitution of Mrs. Canning in her place.

When the girl had first arrived in England he had foreseen the possibility that sooner or later it would be necessary for her to go the same way as her uncle, and he had searched round for someone sufficiently like her to assist him in his scheme. In Mrs. Canning he had found the person he sought. She was the wife of a man over whom Gates had a hold, and it was easy to force her to do his bidding. The scheme was well-nigh perfect, and, but for an accident, might easily have succeeded.

'I never thought there was such a thing as a great criminal,' commented Farringdon Street, when the whole of Sam Gates's schemes had been laid bare, 'but he certainly was one. He possessed the organising power of a Napoleon. In legitimate business he might have become a millionaire.'

'He must have been nearly that as it was,' grunted Hallick. 'The money he made out of the estate was enormous.'

Farringdon sighed. 'I shall have to try something of the sort myself,' he remarked.

The inspector looked at him. 'Why?' he asked. 'What do you want to become a millionaire for?'

The reporter reddened, and a look of understanding came into Hallick's eyes.

'Oh, I see.' He whistled softly. 'Yes, she'll have a lot of money, Street. A hell of a lot of money! More than the finest reporter in the world could ever earn.'

'I'm afraid you're right, Hallick,' said Farringdon. 'Well, I've got the satisfaction of knowing that I did my bit towards her getting it.' He sighed again, and then, changing the subject: 'I'm sorry for that poor girl, Pamela Earnshaw. She was terribly cut up at the news of her father's death.'

'You needn't be sorry for her,' grunted Hallick. 'She's marrying young Holt next month.'

'Marrying him!' Farringdon stared his astonishment. 'Why, they've only met three times.'

'He's an American,' said the inspector, 'and 'hustle' is their motto!'

THE END